She'd reached him.

She was right by him. Her arm was brushing his.

She glanced sideways up at him.

Mistake.

The smile had faded. He was looking down at her with such an expression…

She stopped. Of course she stopped. When a man was looking at a woman as Dev was looking at her...

'Dev.'

'I can't,' he told her, and she felt her heart twist within. His words held a pain that was well nigh unbearable.

'I'm just a woman, Dev,' she said softly. 'What's the problem?'

Marion Lennox was born on an Australian dairy farm. She moved on—mostly because the cows weren't interested in her stories! Marion writes Medical Romance™ as well as Tender Romance™. Initially she used different names, so if you're looking for past books search also for author Trisha David. In her non-writing life Marion cares (haphazardly) for her husband, kids, dogs, cats, chickens and anyone else who lines up at her dinner table. She fights her rampant garden (she's losing) and her house dust (she's lost!). She also travels, which she finds seriously addictive. As a teenager Marion was told she'd never get anywhere reading romance. Now romance is the basis of her stories, her stories allow her to travel, and if ever there was one advertisement for following your dream she'd be it! You can contact Marion at www.marionlennox.com

Recent titles by the same author:

RESCUED BY A MILLIONAIRE
   (Tender Romance)
THE DOCTOR'S SPECIAL TOUCH
   (Medical Romance)
THE DOCTOR'S RESCUE MISSION
   (Medical Romance)
THE LAST-MINUTE MARRIAGE
   (Tender Romance)

BRIDE BY ACCIDENT

BY
MARION LENNOX

MILLS & BOON®

With grateful thanks to Mr David Deutscher
for Katy's splenectomy. Any errors are mine alone.
Thanks also to Ms Anne Gracie
and the late Lord Bromford for providing me with
laughter, encouragement and my ducklings.

All the characters in this book have no existence outside
the imagination of the author, and have no relation
whatsoever to anyone bearing the same name or names.
They are not even distantly inspired by any individual
known or unknown to the author, and all the incidents
are pure invention.

First published in Great Britain 2005
Large Print edition 2006
Harlequin Mills & Boon Limited,
Eton House, 18-24 Paradise Road,
Richmond, Surrey TW9 1SR

© Marion Lennox 2005

ISBN 0 263 18863 9

Set in Times Roman 15¼ on 16½ pt.
17-0406-55376

Printed and bound in Great Britain
by Antony Rowe Ltd, Chippenham, Wiltshire

CHAPTER ONE

HE WAS here.

Just as she saw him in her dreams, he was beside her. His face was more deeply tanned than she remembered. Laughter lines were deeply etched at the corners of his eyes.

She couldn't remember laughter lines.

He had a lovely face, she thought mistily, struggling through the fog of returning consciousness. Strong. Seemingly almost chiselled. His eyes were the same deep, impenetrable grey she'd fallen in love with the moment he'd smiled at her. And his gorgeous mouth. He'd kissed so well, before... before...

The fog receded. He couldn't be here.

But he was. His eyes weren't smiling, but she hadn't expected that. Not any more. She could scarcely remember the time when those eyes hadn't been clouded in despair.

But something was different. He was looking at her in concern. As if it was possible for him to care.

It was she who should be concerned. She was the one who cared. She'd loved him to despair and back again.

She'd lost.

But now, magically, he was here. His hands were gripping hers as he tried to make her focus. She could feel the warmth of him. The strength.

The strength?

'Corey,' she murmured, but his face didn't change. Still there was a concern that she didn't recognise—didn't understand.

'Is your breathing OK?' he asked. 'Does it hurt to breathe?'

It wasn't Corey. The voice wasn't the same. It was deeper. Older?

What cruel joke was this?

She was so confused. She tried to make herself speak, but it was so hard.

'Let me be,' she murmured. 'I'll be fine, Corey. I'm always fine.'

A voice called then from behind them. It was another voice she didn't know, loud and male and fearful.

'You've gotta come, Doc.'

It was over. The dream was receding, as she knew it must. Corey—her Corey—put a hand on her forehead and smoothed her dark curls back from her face.

'Lie still,' he told her. 'Help's coming.'

Sure.

*   *   *

It was the sort of disaster every doctor dreaded.

Dr Devlin O'Halloran rose from the woman he'd been checking and stared around, trying desperately to decide where to go next. The woman was dazed but her breathing was fine, which was all he had time to check. Everything else had to wait.

Triage. Priorities. The problem was there was only one doctor—him—and this disaster might well need a dozen.

This place was so isolated.

Karington National Park, a Queensland paradise where rainforest met sea, was said to be one of the most beautiful places in the world. The locals who lived here loved it. Tourists thought it was magic.

But the steep cliffs and high mountains meant that the roads here were treacherous, especially at the end of the rainy season when the roadsides were sodden and liable to crumble. The logging truck had come around the bend too fast. One logging truck with an unstable load meeting one school bus with twenty kids on board.

And one tiny, two-seater car with a pregnant driver.

These trucks weren't supposed to use this route, Dev thought savagely. It might be more direct than the inland road, but it was far more dangerous. By the look of it, the truck had swerved to miss the car. It hadn't, quite. It had clipped the front, then slammed into the cliff. The logs had been thrown off with force, and they'd rolled down against the school bus. The logs were vast eucalypts from the farmed timberlands north of the national park. They'd crushed the side of the bus and they'd pushed it sideways off the road.

Towards the sea thirty feet below.

They were desperately lucky that the bus hadn't slid right down. Now it was lying on its side, balanced precariously on the cliff face.

Likely to slide further.

This was chaos.

He couldn't cope.

Dev had been at a house call only minutes from here when the call had come. An emergency transmitter on the bus console—installed because one of the schoolkids was a severe asthmatic—was linked directly to Dev's cellphone. Jake had obviously hit the transmit button and yelled that he was needed. Nothing else. The transmission had ended before he'd got details. So Dev had headed along the bus route, expecting an asthma attack, swearing at Jake for not telling him more.

And found this.

Chaos.

There was no one but him.

The truck driver was sitting on the roadside, shocked into immobility. Jake, the local bus driver, was staring at the bus as if he couldn't believe what was happening.

Children were clambering out the back window of the bus—using it as an emergency exit. Someone seemed to be lifting them out from the inside. They were helping each other down.

Jake was useless.

The bus could slide at any minute.

'Jake, will you help get these kids out?' he snapped. 'I want everyone off the bus—now.'

Why hadn't Jake already done it? It had been almost five minutes since he'd called.

There were ten or twelve kids on the verge now, clustered in a shocked, confused huddle.

There were still more on the bus. If it slid…

It mustn't slide. Not yet.

He was helping the kids down from the back windows now, hauling them out, swinging them down to the roadside, giving each a cursory check as he went. The children were battered, bleeding, crying, but there was no time for comfort. He'd practically fallen over the young woman so he'd checked her first, but getting the kids out had to be the highest priority.

Damn, why hadn't Jake done this before anything? he thought as he realised just how precariously the bus was balanced. The man must be more shocked than he'd thought.

Maybe he was lucky Jake had had the capacity to call him at all.

The kids were still emerging, sliding out into his arms as he lifted them down. Some were crying, but most were so shocked they were simply following instinct. They were from the local primary school—kids aged between six and twelve.

He needed help. He had to get more help.

He had to keep pulling kids out. The bigger ones were out now but someone inside was handing the littlies out to him. The teacher?

'Come on, you can do it. You must.'

Yeah. The teacher. Colin Jeffries. Devlin recognised his voice, giving shaky directions from inside.

'I think…I've got all I can,' Colin called, his voice wavering. 'There's a couple more trapped but I can't…I can't… And Jodie's in real trouble.'

'OK, come out yourself,' Dev called.

Colin did, sliding awkwardly backwards out through the bus's rear window—the emergency exit that was the only way anyone could get out. Dev moved to help him. In his mid-fifties, his suit ripped and spattered with blood, Colin was bleeding profusely from a deep gash on his face, and he was hauling a kid out after him.

'Jodie needs help,' he told Dev, and he laid Jodie down at Devlin's feet before sitting—abruptly—himself.

There was blood everywhere. Far too much blood.

Some of it was the schoolteacher's. More than enough to tip him over into unconsciousness, Dev thought grimly.

But the child's blood was pumping. Triage. Jodie.

'Get some pressure on your head,' Dev snapped at Colin. 'Put both hands against the bleeding and push—hard.'

He was doing the same himself, pressing hard against Jodie's shoulder. Hell, he had to stop this.

But there was so much need.

Priorities.

There were kids all around him, milling, seeing him as the only authority figure.

'Jake?' he called, but the bus driver didn't respond. The driver was staring at the bus as if he was seeing something he'd never seen before.

Dev didn't even have time to shake him back to reality.

OK. There was only him. He raised his voice as he worked over Jodie. Most of these kids had been his patients for the three years he'd been practising medicine in the town. He knew their parents from childhood. They knew him.

'Can the oldest—Katy and Marty, that must be you—collect the kids together? Sit everyone down well away from the bus. We'll get your parents here soon. But first, Marty, can you run and get my bag from the back seat of my car? It's not locked. Run.'

That was all he had time for. He wasn't looking at the kids. Or at the teacher. This was Jodie— Jodie McKechnie, a tiny ten-year-old who he knew well, and her situation was desperate.

There was blood pumping from her shoulder. Bright arterial blood.

It had to be a torn artery.

Jake was still standing immobile. Helpless.

There was no time here for helplessness.

'Jake, grab my phone.' He gestured to his belt and then as Jake stared at him as if he didn't know what he was talking about, he yelled. 'Jake, grab the phone. Now!'

Jake moved. Trancelike.

There was no time for sympathy. 'Call the hospital,' he snapped. 'I want every available person at the hospital out here now. Tell them that. And then help get those kids clear. Colin says there's still kids on the bus. You have to get them off. You must.'

But that was all he had time for. Jodie. He was losing Jodie.

Hell, he needed pressure. He'd have to clamp blood vessels. He had to stop this bleeding.

There was still chaos around him.

But he could only do what he could manage now. If he didn't stop the bleeding within minutes, Jodie would be dead.

Marty appeared at his side with his doctor's bag—already open—and Devlin blessed him.

'Help Katy now,' he told him.

That was all he had time for. He blocked out the remaining chaos. He had one child to care for.

He had one life in his hands and he could think of nothing else.

Emma lifted her head with extreme caution. What on earth had happened?

Where was she?

She stared around her, stunned. Cautiously she pushed herself to a sitting position, willing the fog to clear so she could finally figure out what must have happened.

There'd been a crash. There must have been a crash.

But she couldn't remember. All she knew was that she was sprawled on the road. She remembered lying still, trying to make her head work, exploring every piece of her body, unable to believe that she was still alive.

Until the voice had arrived. The face. She remembered the face.

The face above her had cemented her feeling that she was in some other space. Not here. Not in reality. The face was her husband's.

And Corey was dead.

No. He wasn't dead. He was here.

Maybe she was dead.

No, she told herself fiercely, trying hard to get a grip on reality.

Corey was dead. She wasn't.

Someone was snapping orders, fast, harsh. The man she'd thought was Corey?

Someone was crying. A child. It was a thin, fragile sobbing and it helped her haul herself together. It helped ground her.

The fog receded, just a little.

She'd definitely been in a car smash. This was real.

Somewhere a child was terrified. Did that mean she had to pull herself together and do something about it?

She put her hand to her head and felt, gingerly, all over. Ouch. OK, she'd been hit on the head and maybe she'd been out of it for a minute or so. But she was OK. She was fine.

She moved her head a little and paused.

All right, not fine. But she was OK, and OK was all she had to be going on with.

But this wasn't just her. She put a hand on her bulge and thought in sudden fierce anxiety, My baby has to be OK, too.

As if in response she felt a kick, for all the world like an indignant reminder that she should take more care of her precious cargo.

'Hey, this wasn't my fault,' she told her bulge as she pushed herself up onto knees that were decidedly jelly-like.

She used the car—her mangled car—to haul herself higher. To her feet.

Her car was a mangled wreck. She'd been lucky to get out alive.

She was alive. What next?

The face had said to lie still.

How could she?

The child's sobbing was a trickling stream of fear. What had the professor said at the kids' hospital where she'd done her medical internship? If a kid comes through the front door screaming, he can usually be put at the end of the queue. It's the quiet ones you look at first. Don't ignore the quiet ones.

Did that mean she could ignore the sobbing?

No. This sobbing wasn't a hysterical scream. It was a sound of pure terror.

Where was the face? Where was the man she'd thought was Corey?

What had happened?

She stared around her, growing more appalled by the minute.

There were logs everywhere, vast, bare trunks, each maybe two feet thick and twenty feet long. They were sprawled over the road like bowled ninepins.

A guy—maybe the truck driver?—was retching over on the verge.

Another guy—a little man with a white face and a ripped shirt—was frantically punching numbers into a mobile phone.

A third adult was crouched by the lorry, clutching his head. There was a crimson stain blooming under his hands.

And then there were the children.

One of the children was lying on the road and someone else—another man, the face?—was working frantically over him. Over her?

Her. A girl.

The little girl was wearing pink tights, stained crimson. There was a medical bag spread open and she could see the face was trying to attach clamps.

He looked so like Corey, she thought, the fog drifting. If he was Corey then he must be a doctor, which would explain…

He wasn't Corey. He was an unknown doctor, working desperately to save a life. She was concussed. She was seeing things.

She wasn't imagining the blood. There was far too much blood.

She could help. She took a step towards him and then she paused, her medical training slamming in.

No. This wasn't about one child. She had to figure out priorities.

Triage.

Somehow she forced her attention from the doctor and his small patient. Her eyes started moving methodically from child to child, assessing as she went.

These kids had all obviously clambered or been lifted from the wreck of the bus. Scratches, lacerations, shock. She did a visual check of each child as well as she could. Looking for desperate need.

Damn, why didn't her legs want to hold her up?

They had to. They had no choice.

The guy with the bloody head—an older guy in a suit—was looking as if he was in real trouble. He was sitting by the bus as if he'd collapsed there.

Maybe she should go to him first.

His situation didn't look immediately life-threatening.

Assess the whole situation.

The kids were all moving. No one seemed to be unconscious. There was lots of blood, but nothing that looked like uncontrolled bleeding. A couple of children were cradling their arms. There'd be fractures, she thought. Lacerations.

Her eyes moved swiftly across the group. Nothing too urgent, she thought, moving on.

OK, go to the guy with the suit and the bloody head, or help the doctor.

Maybe that was where she was needed most. She could help the doctor with the clamps. There was so much blood. He was fighting against the odds.

But still she held back. This whole assessment had taken only seconds. She'd checked the people. Now assess the scene for further danger.

Her training—taking in the whole situation before deciding on action—made her eyes move on. To the bus. It lay precariously on the cliff edge, with logs pushing against it. The doctor must have been moving to the bus to check it, she thought, and then been deflected by a need that had been even more urgent. A child bleeding to death.

The bus could slide down.

Was it empty? It had to be empty.

How to check?

She forced her feet to walk across to the guy with the phone. Somehow. Her legs really didn't want to hold her up.

The guy looked as if he was trying to make a phone call. He was punching numbers.

'Is everyone out of the bus?' she asked.

He turned and stared at her as if he didn't understand what she was saying. As if she was a voice without a body attached. Then, without answering, he turned back to the phone and started punching numbers again.

Too many numbers. The job was too much for him. His fingers were all over the place. Achieving nothing.

He must be in deep shock.

Who was he trying to ring? Emergency services? Surely someone had rung them.

Here was a priority.

There was no time for gentleness. Emma took a deep breath, told her legs to stay working—she felt as if her body belonged to someone else—and she lifted the phone from the man's nerveless fingers. She didn't have time to treat him with kid gloves. The bus could slide at any minute.

'Is everyone out of the bus?' she demanded, in a voice that could have been heard interstate. It wasn't a voice that could be ignored.

Especially when she was two inches from his face.

He gaped.

But he didn't respond.

She lowered her voice to threatening.

'You want me to slap you? Answer me! Is the bus empty?'

It worked. Sort of. She'd shocked him out of his stupor, but he was still no use. 'N-no,' he whispered. 'I can't... I don't know.'

He reached for the phone again, as if that was all he could think of to do.

Maybe he didn't know whether the bus was empty. Maybe he couldn't even manage a phone call. Emma took a step back, held onto the phone, punched the emergency code and waited until a female voice responded.

'Emergency. What service do you require?' The voice was clinically efficient and Emma blessed her for it. Maybe this call had already been made but she was taking no chances.

'All of them,' she snapped. 'A school bus has been crushed by logs a few miles north of Karington on the coast road. The bus is threatening to slide off the cliff. This guy will give you details but we need every service now, including cranes to secure the bus. I want ambulances, medics, po- lice, heavy machinery to stop the bus from sliding. There may be kids trapped on the bus. Get out the army if you must, but get help for us now.'

She'd done something at least, which was al- most amazing in itself. Her body didn't feel as if it belonged to her.

But she had to go on. She handed the phone back to the dazed bus driver and instructed her legs to walk forward a bit further. To the bus.

That meant she had to pass the guy on the ground treating the little girl. The doctor.

He didn't look up. She looked down and saw what he was doing.

So much blood.

He needed help. To apply pressure and clamp arteries himself...he needed someone else.

But the bus could slide.

He was searching, desperately searching, for blood vessels.

Priorities. Too many children.

She didn't stop. She couldn't. Triage. If there were still kids on the bus and it slid...

She couldn't let herself be deflected.

She'd reached the guy with the bloodied face now—the middle-aged man in a suit. Maybe a schoolteacher? There was blood streaming from a gash on his forehead and she stooped to see, hauling her jacket off to form a pad as she knelt.

'You were on the bus?' she asked, pushing the pad hard over his face. 'Lie down flat.' She pushed him down and started pressing. 'Is everyone off?'

He groaned. 'There's still a couple...I think. I'm not sure but there were a couple of children I couldn't reach. Before...before...'

He wavered. He was suffering from blood loss as well as shock, Emma thought, and he was close to sliding into unconsciousness.

'Stay still,' she told him again, propelling him backwards so he was lying flat. She pushed hard on the pad but she was already looking around to find someone who could take over. It was an ugly gash, deep and ragged, but she had to move on.

The two drivers were useless. Which left only the kids.

He'd have to do this himself.

She guided his hands up to the makeshift pad. 'Push down on this and don't let go,' she told him. 'Push hard.'

It was the best she could do. She straightened— and there was a child beside her. A little girl, who only reached her shoulder. Skinny. Pig tails. Really thick glasses.

About twelve.

'What do you want us to do?' the girl said, matter-of-factly, and Emma could have kissed her. The bus driver and the lorry driver were worse than useless. The teacher was too badly injured to help. She had to use this child.

'What's your name?' she asked.

'Katy.'

'Katy, you're doing great,' Emma told her. 'I need a leader and you're it. Can you organise the big kids to check the little ones? Tell everyone that they need to cuddle anyone who's hurt. Gently. Lay anyone down who needs to lie down and tell other kids to stay with them. Organise everyone into pairs so that everyone has someone who's looking after them. If I find anyone else on the bus, can I send them out to you?'

'Sure. Me and Marty will look after them,' Katy said. 'Do you want someone to push down on Mr Jeffries's pad?'

If there had been a medal to hand, Emma would have pinned it on her right then.

'Yes,' she told her.

'I'll call Chrissy Martin to look after Mr Jeffries while I look after the others,' Katy said. 'She reckons she's going to be a doctor and she doesn't get sick when anyone bleeds.'

'Are all the kids out of the bus?' Please…

'There's two still left,' Katy told her, and Emma forgot about medals. 'Kyle Connor and Suzy Larkin. I was just coming to look for them.' She looked dubiously at the bus. 'You reckon it's safe to go back inside?'

'I'll look for you,' Emma told her, staring with her at the bus with a sinking heart. 'You have work to do.'

So did she.

Someone had to climb into the bus.

Kyle and Suzy. Two children. Two children on the bus.

There was sea under the bus. Thirty feet down. What was stopping the bus from sliding into the sea?

Nothing.

She looked back at the rest of the adults to see if there was anyone who could possibly help her.

Not the doctor. If he left what he was doing…well, he couldn't.

The other adults? One sick, one too stunned to be any use at all, one injured.

Not a snowball's chance in a wildfire of any help from this lot.

She couldn't ask the kids.

Which left her.

She gulped.

'Don't slide,' she told the bus. Stupidly. Inconsequentially. 'Don't you dare slide. I haven't come all this way to get squashed.'

Squashed wasn't a good thought and she couldn't afford to think it. If she hesitated any more she wouldn't do it. There was no choice.

Two kids.

She reached up, grabbed the top of the window-frame and hauled herself up and inside the bus.

She was met by chaos.

A bus, lying on its side at a thirty or forty degree angle on the side edge of a cliff wasn't the most organised place to be at the best of times. And this one had been crushed by rolling logs.

There was shattered glass, twisted metal and seats, satchels spilling schoolbooks…

How had so many kids got out of here alive? Emma asked herself as she tried to get her bearings.

The frame was still almost intact. That'd be why. There'd be cuts from the broken glass but not much impact damage.

What else might have caused major trauma?

There were a couple of logs that had smashed right inside.

Maybe they'd missed everyone.

Yeah, right.

But maybe they had. She couldn't hear anything.

'Is anyone in here?' she called, trying not to sound as terrified as she felt.

Nothing.

Maybe Katy had been mistaken. Please.

She bit her lip—then slid her way slowly down, gingerly, horribly conscious of the fact that the bus was precariously balanced thirty feet above the sea. But there was nothing she could do about that little nightmare. She couldn't think about it.

She did think about it.

No matter. She couldn't let it matter. She worked slowly down the rows of seats, searching, searching…

Thank God she was wearing sensible clothes. Her oversized jeans and windcheater and her sneakers protected her from the worst of the broken glass. If she'd been in summer dress and sandals she'd be have been cut to ribbons.

Where were they?

Katy had said there were two kids. Katy looked the sort of kid who'd miss nothing.

And as she thought it, she found the first.

She almost missed him. A vast log had smashed through a window, crushing the child against the far bus wall. Crushing him so that she could scarcely see him. The log had rolled back as the bus had settled, but Kyle had been left where he'd been crushed.

No.

He must have died instantly, Emma thought, sickened beyond belief. A little boy, seven or eight…

Bright copper hair.

Dead.

She swallowed and swallowed again. Katy had said his name was Kyle.

Kyle.

She was crying now. Tears were sliding uselessly down her cheeks and she couldn't stop them. She didn't try.

'Kyle.' She whispered his name, then put her hand across to touch the little boy's face. His face was almost untouched but the rest of him… No. She checked for a pulse, but it was no use. She was searching for something she knew had irretrievably gone.

Useless.

Her touch turned into a tiny gesture of blessing. It was all she could do for him.

Doctors should grow accustomed to death.

Doctors never did.

Two kids. She had to move on. Katy had said there were two kids. She swiped away the useless tears and went on searching.

Where…? Had someone been thrown out?

Where?

'Suzy?' she called.

Nothing.

She was reaching the front of the bus now, the lowest point—checking, checking.

And then she heard…

It was a rasping, choking sound, so slight it had been almost lost in the sounds she herself was making as the broken glass crunched under her.

Where had the sound come from?

Further forward.

Here.

She paused, staring down in horror.

Suzy.

The little girl had been hit. Not like Kyle—she hadn't been completely crushed. But the log had slammed against her face.

Her eyes were OK. She was staring upward, frantic. Caught between two seats, she hadn't been able to call for help.

Of course she hadn't. It was all she could do to breathe, Emma realised, sliding down so she was right against her. Every breath was a gurgling, gasping attempt to gain enough air to survive.

She was failing. There was a dreadful hue to her skin, which was mute evidence that her efforts weren't enough.

The log had smashed her cheek, her mouth, her throat. The damaged flesh would be swelling, making breathing more difficult every second.

'It's OK,' Emma told her, catching her hands and trying to sound assured, not panicked. 'You're OK, now, Suzy. I'm a doctor. I'm here to help you breathe. It's OK.'

The child stared wildly up at her, her eyes reflecting the terror that Emma felt.

And then, as if she'd held on for long enough— for too long—she fought for one last dreadful breath and she slipped into unconsciousness.

No.

Unconsciousness meant death, Emma thought desperately. Without fighting, how could Suzy get air past the damage? How could she get the oxygen she so desperately needed?

Emma slipped her fingers into the little girl's throat, frantically hoping that she might find loose teeth or bloody tissue that could be cleared. What she felt there made her lift her fingers back in despair. It wasn't just loose teeth or blood blocking the trachea. This was major damage. Air wasn't going to get into these lungs via the child's mouth or nose.

What next?

The guy outside had a doctor's bag. He'd have a scalpel, maybe a tracheostomy tube…

No. It'd take too long to call—explain—get the bag in here. The child was dying under her hands.

She had seconds.

The breathing was a rasping, thin whistle, each one shorter than the last. The little girl's body was convulsing as she fought for breath.

The fight was lost.

She had to do something now! She stared wildly round. What? Anything. Anything.

A child's pencil-case…

She hauled it open, ripping at the zip so hard it broke. What? What?

A pencil sharpener. A ballpoint pen.

She hauled them out, sobbing in desperation. Maybe.

She had her fingernail in the tiny screw of the sharpener, twisting, praying, and the tiny screw moved in her hands. In seconds she had the screw out, and the tiny blade of the sharpener slid free into her palm.

She had a blade. A crazy, tiny blade but a blade. Dear God. Now she needed a tracheostomy tube.

She hauled the ink tube from the ballpoint.

OK, so now she had basic equipment. Sort of.

How sharp was her blade?

There was no time to ask any more questions. It was this or nothing. Suzy was jerking towards death.

Go.

And in seconds it was done—the roughest, most appalling tracheostomy Emma was ever likely to see, ever likely to perform, in her life.

Where was her medical training now? Was she mad?

To cut an incision in Suzy's throat with a rough blade from a pencil sharpener, to insert a ballpoint casing that still had ink stains and teeth marks on the end where its owner had thoughtfully chewed while doing his schoolwork—how could it possibly work?

But wonderfully, magically, it did. Within seconds of the ballpoint casing entering her rough incision site, Suzy's breathing rerouted through the plastic.

The awful, non-productive gasping ceased.

The child was still unconscious but her breathing was settling to a rhythm. The dreadful blue was fading.

She'd done it. She relaxed, just for a moment.

The bus shifted, lurched, and she forgot about relaxing.

For a moment she thought they'd plummet together and all she thought was, What a waste. What a waste of a truly amazing piece of surgery.

She'd succeeded, she thought wildly, terror and jubilation crazily mixed. Suzy could live. There was no way this bus could plummet now.

'Let's just keep really still,' she told herself. Not that she had a choice. She was holding the ballpoint casing right where it had to be held. If she moved, Suzy's breathing would stop. As simple as that.

She couldn't move.

The little girl's eyes flickered open, and Emma put her spare hand on the child's forehead to stop her jerking as she regained consciousness.

'Suzy, you're fine. But you mustn't move. I've put a tube in your throat to help you breathe but you mustn't move an inch. Not an inch.'

The child's eyes widened.

Emma was right there.

'I'm not moving either, Suzy,' she told her. 'We're stuck on the bus and we're waiting for someone to come and get us out. Who do you think will come first? I'd like the fire brigade. Wouldn't you? All those bells and sirens sound great, and I love firemen's helmets.'

Suzy's eyes said she was crazy. Maybe she was crazy.

'What shall we do while we wait?' Emma continued, still holding Emma's forehead firmly. 'Maybe I should introduce myself. I'm Emma O'Halloran. I'm a doctor from England and I'm here to meet my baby's extended family. Only they don't know I exist. Do you think they'll be pleased to learn about my baby?'

When help came it came as a cavalry.

Daphne, the lady in charge of Karington's telephone emergency response, had rung everyone she could think of. Emma had said send the army and Daphne hadn't done that, but only because there wasn't an army to hand. She'd sent everyone else.

The sirens were faint at first, but they built until it sounded as if the entire emergency services for the country were heading this way.

Devlin had Jodie's bleeding stopped—almost. He was concentrating now on setting up an intravenous line. He had to get fluids into Jodie's little body if she wasn't to die of shock. Given the amount of blood loss, heart failure was a real possibility.

He had his jacket off, and it was spread over the child to keep her warm. He set the drip to maximum—saline and plasma. Thank God he never travelled without them. Even so, his supplies were severely limited. So, as the cavalry arrived, the relief he felt was almost overwhelming.

The local ambulance was the first to appear. As the two paramedics, Helen and Don, parked their vehicle and ran across to meet him, he decided that he'd never been more grateful to see anyone in his life.

There was no time for greetings. 'I need more plasma here,' he said curtly. 'And I need her warmed. Do you have warmed blankets on board?'

Helen, the senior officer, looked down at Jodie and nodded.

'Yep. Will do. But it looks like you've done the hard part.' She knelt and placed her stethoscope on Jodie's chest and listened—something Devlin hadn't had time to do. But what she heard was obviously reassuring. 'It's sounding steady,' she told him. 'Don, can you take over here? Dev, what else?'

Thank heaven for Helen, Devlin thought. In her early fifties, Helen had been born and bred a dairy farmer. But after her husband died in a tractor accident and her kids left home for the city, she'd retrained as an ambulance officer. Her decision to turn to medicine meant Karington had an ambulance team second to none.

What else? She was asking for the next priority and he hadn't had time to think of one.

But it was staring them both in the face. Sort of. The quarter of it they could see above the clifftop.

'The bus,' he started, and then paused. As if his mention of it had caused a reaction, the bus gave a long, rolling shudder—as though it was about to topple.

Helen made a move towards it but Devlin held her back.

'I think everyone's out.'

'They're not all out.'

It was the child, Katy. She was crouched on the roadside beside her schoolteacher, pressing Emma's jacket against the gash on his head as Emma had shown her. Now she looked up, her eyes filling with tears that it seemed she'd been holding back until now. Somehow.

'The pregnant lady's on the bus,' she told them. 'I told her that Kyle and Suzy were still on the bus and she climbed in after them. She hasn't come out. I told her that Chrissy would do this, but Chrissy was sick so I have to do it. But I don't know what the pregnant lady's doing.'

Devlin did a fast sift of available information. 'The pregnant lady?'

How many pregnant ladies could there be? His eyes moved to the woman he'd seen first—the woman who'd been lying beside her crushed car. He'd almost fallen over her as he'd run.

Her car was still there. Of course. It was mangled past repair.

The woman wasn't.

He'd thought she was only semi-conscious.

How could she be on the bus? He'd told her to lie still. She looked as if she could have been badly injured.

But it had been such a fleeting impression. She was a young woman, he thought, and she'd been badly battered in the crash. She had dark curls, bunched back with ribbon, big green eyes that were too big for her shocked, white face, a smear of blood on her forehead.

She'd been pregnant. Very pregnant.

She needed medical attention.

'She's on the bus?' he said again, blankly.

'Yes,' Katy told him, still fighting back tears of reaction 'I was going to get on and look for Kyle and Suzy myself, but she told me I had to look after Mr Jeffries and the younger kids. She said she'd go. But…she hasn't come out. Do you think it's going to fall?'

She started to cry.

CHAPTER TWO

'IS THERE someone inside?'

The call echoed through the smashed bus and no words had ever sounded sweeter.

Emma had listened to the sirens approaching. She'd heard vehicles stop, people talking, urgent voices, kids crying. And now there was a voice, calling through the shattered back window. It was the voice of the man she'd thought was Corey.

It wasn't Corey. She must have been stupid to think it was.

Whoever it was, at least it was help.

'They're here,' she told Suzy.

Suzy couldn't answer. Of course she couldn't. But the little girl's bravery defied description. She was following orders to the letter, not moving a fraction. Her eyes were locked onto Emma's, and Emma knew that contact was dreadfully important.

So was the contact Emma's fingers were making. She was holding the ballpoint as if it was the most precious thing in the world. As indeed it was. It was the fine thread between life and death.

And now it seemed as if life might just win. Might…

'We're in here,' she called, trying to make her voice assured. Mature. In charge. 'Suzy and I are here, just waiting for rescue. We're hoping for the fire brigade.'

There was a moment's hesitation.

'Is Kyle in there with you?'

Lightness faded. There was no way to dress this up to make it less brutal. She tightened her grip on Suzy's forehead, and forced herself to respond.

'Kyle's been crushed,' she said flatly. 'He's dead. He must have died instantly.'

There was a moment's silence. An awful silence while those outside the bus took in the awfulness.

Then another question, as if he was afraid to ask.

'Is Suzy OK?'

'She'll be fine,' Emma said, forcing her voice to sound firm and sure. 'But we've had some problems. I've performed a tracheostomy. I'm holding a ballpoint casing in position to help her breathe. We can't move.'

There was an even longer silence at that.

'You've performed a tracheostomy?'

'Yes. Her face has been badly hurt. But she'll be fine, just as soon as you can get her out of here.'

'Who the hell are you?'

'Emma.' What did he want? she thought grimly. Proof of medical qualifications?

'You're the pregnant lady who was driving the Kia?'

'That's me.' She smiled down at Suzy and tried again to force lightness into her voice. 'So there's me, there's my bulge and there's Suzy. We'd appreciate it if you could get us out as soon as possible. Please.'

'We'll do our best.' There were sounds of an argument outside the bus but she couldn't make out exactly what was being said. A few voices, mixed.

'Miss?' It was another voice. Lower. Deeper. Different.

'Yes?'

'I'm Greg Nunn from the fire brigade.'

That was good news.

'We hoped the fire brigade would come,' Emma said, speaking to Suzy as much as to the voice outside. 'If we have a fire engine, then we think that anything's possible. We're very pleased to hear from you, Mr Nunn. Suzy and I were hoping we might get rescued by the fire brigade—and here you are.'

Only they weren't quite close enough. 'We can't come in,' Greg told her. 'No one can until the bus is secure. This bus isn't too stable.'

Her smile faded a bit. Not too stable...

'We know that,' she said in some asperity. 'What are you going to do about it?'

'Can you lift the little girl out?'

'I told you, I can't. First, we're right down at the front of the bus and I'm not very good at climbing and lifting. Second, I'm holding a tracheostomy tube in place.'

'Can you come out yourself?'

He had to be joking.

'No,' she said flatly.

'If she's holding a tracheostomy tube in place, she can't,' the first voice said. The doctor?

'Who are you?' she asked—and it was suddenly absurdly important that she knew. He had a doctor's bag. He had to be a doctor.

She could really use a doctor right now.

'I'm Devlin O'Halloran,' he told her. 'Dr O'Halloran.'

She froze.

Things were swinging away from her again. The sensation of dizziness she'd fought ever since her car had been struck came sweeping back, and for a horrible moment she thought she might pass out.

Devlin O'Halloran.

Was this someone's idea of a sick joke?

Corey. Devlin. Of course.

It wasn't a joke.

'I can't come on board,' he told her, and his voice sounded strained to breaking point. 'We can't put extra weight inside. We're working to secure the bus now.'

'That's good,' she managed, but her tone must have changed.

'Are you sure you're all right?' he demanded, then, as an aside, added, 'Damn, I'm going in.'

'You go in and the whole thing goes down the cliff,' she heard someone say. 'It doesn't need any more weight. Get real, Doc. We're working as hard as we can.'

Forget the O'Halloran bit, she decided. Her brain was working on so many levels it was threatening to implode from overuse.

She couldn't think about the O'Halloran thing. She didn't want to look around the bus—she mustn't. She had to keep positive—keep hopeful— so that she could remain smiling down at Suzy as if she really believed things were fine.

'What's happening out there?' she called.

This was surreal. She was kneeling by Suzy it was as if they were in a cave and the rest of the world didn't exist. She could hear the sea below them, the waves crashing against the cliffs.

It was a normal sunny day. There were shafts of sunlight piercing the shattered windows. Fifteen minutes ago this had been a glorious morning.

If she looked downwards she could see the sea through the smashed windows. This was wild country and the wind was rising. The sea here was a maelstrom of white foam against the cliffs. Waiting…

'We're attaching cables to the bus,' someone called. 'To get you steady.'

'That's a good idea.'

'But we don't have enough cable,' someone else called. 'We've sent for some from the town. We need steel cables to attach to the trees, and the only trees strong enough are along the cliff a bit.'

'But we've hooked a rope on the fire-engine,' someone else called. 'That should help.'

'Not enough to let Doc down into the bus,' someone else called. 'The road surface isn't stable enough. But we're working fast.'

'Work faster,' she said faintly. 'We like the idea of the fire-engine but Suzy and I are running out of things to talk about.'

It took half an hour. Half an hour while Suzy's throat swelled even more, and it became more and more difficult to keep the plastic tubing right where it had to be. There was bleeding into the wound and a couple of times her breathing faltered.

Emma lifted her a little, cradling on her knees so her head was slightly elevated. She watched her like a hawk, and as her breathing faltered she moved, adjusted, adjusted...

Somehow she kept her breathing.

She must be in such pain. The child lay limply in Emma's arms and stared up at Emma her as if the link to this strange lady above her was the only thing between her and death.

Which wasn't so far from the truth, Emma thought, as the minutes dragged on.

The ballpoint casing couldn't last for ever.

Hurry.

But finally the cable arrived. She heard shouts, barked orders as the men and women outside finally had something to do.

And then…

'She's secure. We're coming on board.'

'Don't wait for an invitation,' she called, and she knew that her voice was starting to wobble. 'Come on in. And bring morphine.'

'We're coming now.'

Two of them came on board. The doctor—Devlin?—and a middle-aged lady in khaki overalls with an ambulance insignia.

They crawled into the bus the same way Emma had come in. She cradled Suzy and watched them come—but only with her peripheral vision. She was still looking down at Suzy, aware that the eye contact she had with the little girl had assumed immense importance.

'They're coming, Suzy,' Emma whispered. 'The cavalry. Dr Devlin O'Halloran and friend.' She glanced up at the approaching figure—a big man in a loose pullover and jeans. Someone had given him leather work gloves. He had a thatch of deep black hair, wavy, sort of flopping over his eyes as if he was in need of a good haircut. He looked so like…

No. He didn't look like anyone, she told herself fiercely. No one she could think of right now.

'I guess this must be your local doctor,' she told Suzy. 'Do you know him?'

But Suzy's eyes were blank. Glazing a little. Shock and pain and blood loss were all taking their toll.

'Have you brought fluids and morphine?' she demanded. That was what she needed most.

'We have.'

Dev had paused momentarily by Kyle—just momentarily. Emma hadn't looked that way again. Not once. But she knew what he'd be seeing and she heard in his voice how much he hated it.

'We've brought everything we need,' Devlin said, but the inflexion in his voice was odd. He wasn't commenting on Kyle. He didn't have to.

'There's nothing we can do here,' he said to the woman with him, and it was almost a sigh. He started to clamber lower.

Helen remained with Kyle, her face closing in distress. 'I'll call in a stretcher for Kyle,' Helen said, as Dev fought his way over the upended seats to reach Emma and Suzy. 'Unless you need me there. Do you?'

'Go ahead,' Devlin said grimly. And then he paused.

He'd reached them. He saw—and his face grew almost incredulous as he saw the situation they were in. As he saw Emma's makeshift attempt at a viable tracheostomy. 'How the hell—?'

'Don't ask questions,' Emma said, fighting off faintness once more. 'I want morphine and intravenous fluid and I want it now.'

'But…'

She didn't have time to listen to buts. 'The ballpoint's secure enough,' she said grimly. 'For now. But we need to work fast.'

A stunned pause.

'Yes, ma'am,' he said. He cleared a flat spot to put his bag and hauled it open, with another fast, incredulous glance at Emma. Then he started work.

'It'll be a couple of minutes before we have Suzy ready to shift,' he told Helen. 'Go ahead and lift Kyle free. I'll manage here. I think. Or rather, *we* will.'

It was a dreadful place to work. An impossible angle. Far too much broken glass. Seats that were upside down. Suzy was lying on the outside wall of the bus, jammed against the bus wall and two seats. Over the last half-hour Emma had wiggled so she was right in there beside her, supporting her head as best she could. It was impossibly cramped.

Dev had taken the situation in at a glance. Emma underneath the little girl, her fingers holding the ballpoint tube.

'I can't move,' Emma said—unnecessarily—and Dev nodded.

'Don't.' He smiled down at Suzy, a slow, lazy smile that almost reassured Emma. Almost. 'You guys just stay still while I do my stuff,' he told them. He wouldn't be sure if Suzy was hearing him but he wasn't taking chances.

'Suzy, I'm giving you something for the pain right now,' he told her. 'Then I'm going to put a little tube in your arm so we can replace some of the blood you've lost. As soon as you stop hurting so much, we'll lift you out of here. Your mum and dad are waiting on the cliff.'

Of course they would be. Emma winced. All the mums and dads would be frantic. By now the rest of the kids would probably have been taken back to town, she thought, and reunited with their parents.

Except for Kyle.

Don't go there.

She was close to breaking, she thought, suddenly fighting another wave of nausea. It was adrenaline that had kept her going until now. But Dev was here and…

'Don't give in now, Emma.' Devlin's voice jerked her back. To the urgency of what she was doing. The dizziness receded. 'Suzy needs you too much.'

'I wasn't planning on giving in,' she said with what she hoped sounded like indignation. 'Only wimps give in.'

'And you're no wimp.'

He sounded teasing, she thought. Nice.

That was another crazy thing to think. Just because he had Corey's face...

No.

He had a syringe prepared now. Swiftly he swabbed Suzy's arm and injected what must be morphine. He wasn't touching her throat. He had too much sense.

'I don't think a stretcher's going to work in here,' he said, glancing at the chaos around them as the morphine slid home. 'That ballpoint needs to stay absolutely still. I don't think taping's going to work.'

'I don't see how it can.' She was lifting the tube a little so it wasn't hitting the far wall of the trachea. A proper tracheal tube would go down, past the damage and the swelling. But to put a proper tracheal tube in now... To remove the ballpoint and to take such a risk...

No. She needed to keep it in place until they got somewhere with decent theatre facilities, where they could operate fast. Where they'd have oxygen to compensate for faltering breathing.

She couldn't leave her ballpoint.

'I think the only way is if we inch her out,' Devlin was saying. He was setting up an IV line, knowing they had to get fluid in. It'd make it more complicated to lift her but they could place the bag on her chest and she needed the fluid so much... 'Literally inch by inch,' he continued. 'If I lift her, can you come with me every step of the way? Can you do that?'

'I can.'

He was looking at her—really looking at her— and there was concern in his face. 'You've been in the accident yourself. You were concussed. You shouldn't be here.'

'I am here. Let's get on with it.'

'I can ask Helen to take over.'

'You can't.'

'Why not?'

'It's taken me time to figure out where this has to lie,' she told him, motioning with her eyes to the ballpoint. 'If I wobble even a fraction from where I'm holding it, it'll block, but I've figured out now how to get it back. I'm the only safe person to hold it.'

He stared at her for a long moment—and then nodded. There was no choice and he knew it.

He went back to fitting the intravenous line. Above them came the sound of scraping, of broken glass being scrunched.

Kyle's stretcher was being hauled from the bus.

'Do you want any more help in here?' Helen sounded subdued—as well she might. She'd helped the stretcher out and then had paused at the window.

'We're going to have to do this on our own,' Devlin told her. 'Just clear a path, Helen, and cross every finger and every toe. And then some.'

He shouldn't ask her for help.

He didn't have a choice.

Dev lifted the little girl carefully, so carefully, inching his way backwards out of the bus. Every move had to be measured so the woman—Emma—could keep up with him. Her hand was holding the ballpoint steady so air could enter Suzy's lungs. She looked so battered he'd been afraid she'd faint, but that battering wasn't affecting her hand. It was rock steady.

Could she keep it up?

Maybe they should stay, he thought. Maybe they should try and stabilise the airway.

To operate in these confines, to remove the ballpoint and try and replace it here…

They couldn't.

It was a huge risk to move Suzy, but it was a risk they had to take. He was forced to depend on this woman he didn't know. This woman who should be a patient herself.

She must be a doctor. She had to be. To perform a tracheostomy in these conditions, with such a result—it was an operation that was little short of miraculous.

But where had she come from? She wasn't a local. Yet tourists didn't tend to travel alone, not when they were six or seven months pregnant.

Now was not the time to ask questions, he decided as he kept inching out. He had Suzy cradled in his arms and Emma was with him every inch of the way.

Just as long as she held up.

He glanced at her face and it was sheet-white. She had the baby to consider, he told himself savagely. She'd been almost unconscious when he'd found her. She should be in hospital herself.

If she were in hospital, Suzy would be dead.

He needed her. Suzy needed her.

He kept inching out backwards.

Emma kept following.

They emerged to a scene that made Emma blink.

The children were gone—all of them. The bus driver, the truck driver, the injured teacher—they were gone, too. They must have been ferried away from the scene at some time while the bus had been in the process of being stabilised. There were two steel cables running from the bus's chassis to the trees on the opposite side of the road.

Since those cables had been attached, they'd been safe.

What else?

Kyle was still there. His tiny, blanket-covered body lay to one side and there was a fireman sitting beside the stretcher. Just sitting. As if he'd sit however long it took. No matter that there was nothing to do. The man's stance said that he was simply here to guard. To begin the grieving for the loss of a tiny life.

Once again Emma felt tears welling behind her eyes.

'Not yet,' the man beside her said, and she blinked.

He knew what she was thinking?

'I'm fine,' she muttered, and he smiled, albeit a shaky one.

'I know you are. You're great.'

There was a stretcher waiting, with Helen hovering. They lay laid Suzy down with care. The morphine had taken hold now and she was drifting in a haze of near-sleep.

'I'll take over now,' Devlin said, moving to take over her grip on the ballpoint, but Emma shook her head.

'I know how it should feel,' she told him. 'I have it right where it should be. I'm hanging on until we get to a proper theatre with proper equipment. And a surgeon. Tell me there's a surgeon at Karington.'

'That would be me,' he said gravely.

That would be him.

Her eyes met his. A surgeon. She had a surgeon right here. The relief was so great it made her dizzy all over again.

'Well, hooray,' she managed. 'So what are we waiting for? Let's find you a theatre and a scalpel and something to replace this blasted pen. But you're not removing me from it except by scalpel.'

And twenty minutes later she was finally, finally able to step away.

Not only was Dev O'Halloran a surgeon, he was a surgeon with real skill. Inserting a tracheostomy tube into a wound that was massively swollen, where the cut was jagged and rough, where there was too much bleeding already and where the patient was a child with a trachea half the size of an adult's... It was a nightmare piece of surgery that Emma couldn't imagine doing. But, then, she couldn't have imagined using a ballpoint casing and a pencil sharpener to perform similar surgery. It seemed that on this day anything was possible.

Devlin's surgery worked. Finally, finally the tube was in place. Emma's ballpoint casing was just an empty piece of plastic abandoned on the tray, and she was free to step back from the table.

They'd used a local anaesthetic. Anything else would have been too risky with the breathing so fragile. But Suzy was so shocked and so groggy with the morphine that she didn't register as Emma stepped back.

'Give the lady a chair,' Devlin growled, and one of the nurses pushed a chair under her legs.

Emma sat.

Her legs felt funny, she thought.

Dev was still working, closing the wound, doing running repairs to the ravages of the little girl's face.

Preparing her for the trip to Brisbane where a skilled plastic surgeon could take over.

She needed to get out of there, Emma decided. Dev had skilled nurses to help him. He no longer needed her.

The smells of the theatre were making her feel ill. She was accustomed to them. They shouldn't…

'Excuse me,' she said, and pushed herself to her feet.

'Go with her, David,' Devlin said urgently to one of the nurses.

'I'll be fine,' she muttered.

But she wasn't.

No matter. She made her jelly legs move.

Ten minutes later, after as nasty a little interlude in the bathroom as she could imagine, she emerged a new woman. Or almost a new woman. She'd washed her face, splashing water over and over until she felt that she was almost back to reality.

What was she about—almost passing out in Theatre?

It was hardly surprising, she told herself. Students did it all the time, and even more experienced theatre staff did it more often than they liked to admit. The trick was to hold it back until you were no longer needed.

She'd done that. She should be proud of herself.

She wasn't.

She swiped some more cold water onto her face and stared into the mirror.

What had she done? Realisation was only just dawning.

She'd risked her baby.

The sight of those cables when she'd climbed from the bus had made her feel sick. She hadn't realised. When she'd climbed on board she'd thought at some superficial level that the bus might slip, but she hadn't considered it as a real possibility. It was only now as she thought back to the huge cables and thought of what might have been…

Her hand dropped to her swollen belly and she flinched.

She'd taken a gamble. She'd won, but such a gamble.

Maybe she wasn't such a new woman. Maybe she'd better splash some more water.

Finally she took a deep breath and went to face the world again. In the waiting room there was a man and a woman—farmers? They looked up as she emerged from the washroom, and their faces reflected terror.

Oh, help. They'd be Suzy's parents, Emma thought. They'd seen her go into Theatre with their daughter, and then they'd seen her rush out to the washroom. Ill.

Two plus two equals disaster.

'Hey, it's fine,' she told them, rushing to take that dreadful look from their faces. 'Everything's gone brilliantly. Suzy's breathing's stabilised and Dr O'Halloran is just fixing the dressings. She'll need to go to Sydney to have her face repaired by a plastic surgeon, but even that doesn't look too difficult. I'd imagine you'll have a Suzy with a couple of scars—but that should be the extent of the damage's all. Honestly.'

The couple visibly restarted their breathing process. Their combined faces sagged in relief.

'But you…'

'I'm pregnant,' she said, trying to make her voice cheerful. 'I'm really sorry I scared you, but pregnant women throw up all the time.'

Their faces cleared still more. 'Oh, my dear…' the woman faltered, and Emma suddenly decided against medical detachment. She bent over and hugged her.

'I know,' she whispered. 'It's been dreadful but now she's safe.'

'We've just seen Kyle's parents,' the man—Suzy's father—said heavily. 'He's the only one dead. We've been lucky, but they...'

'The nurses won't let them see him.' Suzy's mother pulled herself out of Emma's arms and she sniffed. 'But you...you're a doctor.'

'I am.'

'Helen—the ambulance officer—said you saved our daughter's life.'

'I was in the right place at the right time,' she said softly, but Suzy's mother had something else on her mind. Her daughter would make it. She had room to worry now about others.

'The hospital's chief nurse, Margaret Morrisy...she's a stickler for the rules. She's told Kyle's parents that they can't see Kyle until Dr O'Halloran says so. They've been waiting and waiting for Dev to finish and I think...they're going crazy.' She gulped and gave a little nod towards the theatre. 'If it had been Suzy who'd died, then I know what I'd want and I'd want it now. If you're a doctor...can you figure out how they can see him? Now?'

CHAPTER THREE

WHAT she really needed was bed. Urgently. But Emma glanced out to the parking lot and saw Kyle's parents. They were holding each other, isolated, a cocoon of despair that wrenched her far out of her professional detachment and her own need for rest. There were other children around them, staring up at their parents in distress.

A shattered family.

Dev would be in Theatre for another half-hour at least, she thought grimly. He had to make sure Suzy was stabilised for the trip to Brisbane. And then there was everyone else.

Jodie and the schoolteacher—Colin Jeffries—had already been airlifted out. Dev had told her that much. The Medivac air rescue team had blessedly been in the air when they'd sent out a call for help, and they'd been able to evacuate them fast. Jodie needed urgent vascular surgery and Colin's wound required the attention of a plastic surgeon, so they'd taken off straight away, promising to return for Suzy.

That was three patients sorted, but there were so many others. Stitches, fractures, trauma… Dev would be frantic for hours.

Taking care of Kyle's parents would be dreadful, Emma thought, glancing again at the little family out in the parking lot. But maybe she could help. This was something she could do for him.

And she desperately wanted to do something for him, she decided. She thought of Dev as she'd left him in Theatre: a big man with clever fingers and eyes that cared. She let herself dwell on the image for a moment—and she felt the stirring of an emotion that was at least as strong as anything else she'd felt that day.

Dev was like Corey but also unlike him. Gentle yet strong. The way he'd smiled… The way he'd spoken to Suzy…

She caught herself, confused. Where was her mind taking her? This was crazy. She had no business even vaguely thinking of Dev in the way she was thinking of him. It was ridiculous.

She shook away the feeling of unreality she'd had ever since she'd seen Dev. Emotion had to wait. Inexplicable emotion. Inexplicable…linking?

OK, maybe it had to be faced some time but not yet. Meanwhile she had to find the chief nurse.

She found her fast. Margaret was in the nurses' station. Young, very attractive and beautifully presented, her dark hair twisted into an elegant knot, her flawless skin carefully, unobtrusively made up so she seemed perfect, she was speaking urgently into the phone and her tone was one of complete authority.

'I need plasma now. No, it can't wait until morning. Our stocks are completely gone. Well, if you want the risk of an accident in the middle of the night where we can't transfuse—are you personally willing to take that responsibility? I can sign you off on saying that? I didn't think so. I know the Medivac team have already left. No, I shouldn't have asked. I shouldn't have needed to ask. You know what the situation is. I'll leave it to you, then, shall I? Plasma by sunset.'

The phone was replaced.

This was the sort of woman who was invaluable in a crisis, Emma decided. A stickler for rules but ruthlessly efficient. Once onside she'd be an unopposable force.

She needed to get her onside.

'Hi,' Emma said, and the woman came out of the nurses' station to greet her.

'Oh, my dear.' Her voice was warm and decisive. Maybe a little condescending? Surely they had to be about the same age.

No matter.

'We can't believe you've done so much,' she was saying. 'Helen has been telling me what happened. For you to be a doctor, and to be brave enough to climb on the bus… Suzy was so lucky.'

'But not Kyle,' Emma said gently, and Margaret winced.

'I know. It's dreadful.'

'I hear you're not happy about Kyle's parents seeing him until Dr O'Halloran gives the all-clear?'

'No, I—'

'I understand you'd like clearance but I'm happy to take that responsibility.'

'You?' The woman backed off a little.

'I am a doctor.'

'Yes, but…'

'I'm a battered and pregnant doctor, but I'm still a doctor,' Emma said, and her tone was as decisive as Margaret's had been a moment before. 'I can certify death and I can give permission for the relatives to be with him. Kyle's parents need to see him as soon as possible and I can't see any reason for delay. Where is he?'

Margaret was frowning. 'In the morgue.'

'Do you have a private room free?'

'Yes, but—'

'Then let's move him in there, shall we?' she said, her tone still inexorable. 'He's not so dreadfully battered that we risk shock by letting the parents close. Regardless, they need to see him. We both know that. They can't accept his death until they do. So… We need to do the best we can for these people and it can't wait. Can you show me where the morgue is? I'll take care of Kyle's body while you start preparing your private room for him.'

'Can't they see him in the morgue?'

'If he was your little son,' Emma said gently, 'would you like to say goodbye to him in a morgue? I think we can do better than that.'

The log had smashed Kyle's internal organs, crushing him instantly, but to look at his face he might almost be sleeping.

He was such a…

No. Stay dispassionate. Somehow.

Emma washed his face with care. With tenderness. She wrapped his little body tightly so the crushing injuries weren't apparent, she wrapped him again, more loosely, in a soft blanket so if need be he could be lifted and cuddled, and then she supervised the orderlies as they wheeled him through to the ward.

Margaret hovered, anxious, ready to say no, but Emma gave her no chance. She used the authority of her training—and the instincts of her heart. If this little one had been hers…

The orderlies—two young men who looked as if they were barely out of school, and who looked as if the shock of the day had them wanting to be back there—held back, unsure in the face of death, so in the ward it was Emma who lifted him across into the bed, settling his head against the pillows, arranging his features so he wasn't stiffly at attention but rather in the pose of a child sleeping.

Finally she stood back and nodded. She'd done all she could. She couldn't bring him back to life but at least he looked as if he was at peace.

This was so important. Desperately important. In a moment his parents would see him for the last time, and this memory of their child would be carried with them for ever. She couldn't bring him back for them but she could do this.

Finally she went outside to find them. Huddled in their misery, Kyle's parents didn't see her coming. She touched the woman lightly on the shoulder and they turned.

Their children looked mutely up at her, past asking questions.

'Come and see your son,' she told them. 'We've washed him and popped him into a bed for you to say goodbye to him. He's ready.'

'The…kids?' the woman whispered, and Emma looked at the children. At Kyle's brothers and sisters.

'That's up to you,' she said. 'Whether you want your children to say goodbye to their brother is your decision. But if it was my kids…I know what I'd do.'

*   *   *

Fifteen minutes later, Dev left Theatre, reassured Suzy's parents, took two deep breaths and thought, What next?

The Medivac team had taken the worst of the casualties out on the first run.

Suzy was stable and the Medivac helicopter was on its way back to evacuate her. The worst was over.

There'd still be traumatised kids. Too many traumatised kids.

Maybe they could wait for a little. The nurses would have done preliminary assessment and called him for anything urgent.

He needed to find the woman who'd helped him, he thought, and the vision of her as he'd first seen her came back to him. She'd been only semi-conscious. Hell, he'd had no time for her. She'd been injured, yet she'd thrown herself into the chaos and there'd been no time for him to assess her. She'd looked sick as she'd left Theatre.

Kyle. Kyle's parents. They had to be his priority.

But the image of the woman—what had she said her name was, Emma?—stayed with him. She was a heroine, he thought. Somewhere, somehow he'd get a medal for her if he had to do battle with politicians himself to arrange it. She was such a slip of a thing, too thin, her eyes too big for her pinched face, heavy with pregnancy, yet what she'd achieved…

He'd find her. As soon as possible he'd find her.

There was no one at the nurses' station. Where was everyone?

Where was Emma?

There was a sound of distant sobbing. Kyle's family? Margaret came round the corner and met him, her face a mix of uncertainty and concern.

'Kyle's parents?' It must be.

'Kyle's in Room 5,' she told him.

He frowned. The last time he'd seen the child's body the orderlies had been carrying it into the morgue. 'Why?'

'Emma…the doctor…asked me to put him in there so his parents could spend time with him. I hope it's OK. Do you want me to come with you?'

'No,' he told her. 'Do you know where Emma is?'

'She's with them. Or she was.'

What the heck was she doing there? She should be in bed. He needed to check her baby. He…

'You've had a hell of a day,' Margaret was saying. She put a hand on his arm.

He grimaced. 'Yeah,' he said softly, and listened to the sobs. 'But not as hellish as some.'

'I hope I did the right thing, letting Emma bring him from the morgue.'

'Of course.' She seemed to expect it so he gave her a swift hug. She smiled, and then pulled back, smoothing her uniform.

'Not here.'

'No.'

Enough. He had to face Kyle's family.

He turned towards room 5, thinking through the decision to move him. A private room and a bed rather than a stretcher in the morgue. Good call.

Here she was again. His phantom doctor, springing up where he least expected her.

She wasn't very good at lying down and dying, he decided. Thank God.

'OK. It's a good idea,' he told Margaret. 'So you've been talking to her. Do we know anything about her other than her name's Emma?'

'She's bossy,' Margaret said, and gave him a half-smile. 'Almost as bossy as I am. She washed Kyle and made him look…normal. She did a lovely job.'

He winced at that.

A lovely job. Bad choice of words, he told Margaret silently. Was there any such thing as a lovely job where Kyle was concerned?

Kyle was the fourth kid of a family of six and a real little daredevil. Dev had been stitching him up and putting casts on fractured limbs ever since he'd started practising medicine here.

That Kyle was dead was unthinkable.

He was in Room 5. *She'd done a lovely job.*

Deep breath.

Margaret gave him a questioning look, asking him mutely if he wanted her to accompany him, but he shook his head. This was something he had to do by himself.

She left him to it.

He turned into the next corridor—and then paused.

The door to Room 5 was slightly ajar and through the open door he could see Kyle's mother. And Kyle. The woman had lifted her son into her arms and she was cradling him and weeping into his copper curls. Her husband looked on helplessly. Kyle's brothers and sisters were there, too, huddled around their little brother. A family united in grief. A family saying goodbye to their Kyle.

And outside, on the seat outside the door, just out of sight of the family, sat Emma.

She was huddled over, bent at the waist as if she was in pain, and she was weeping silently into her open palms. Her shoulders were racked by silent sobs.

It seemed that Emma had finally stopped.

How long had it been since he'd cradled a woman in his arms?

Never?

Sure, he'd kissed a woman. He and Margaret had a very satisfactory relationship and he thoroughly enjoyed kissing her. But as for cradling her…

He never had. The lines of professional detachment meant that he'd never cradled a patient.

But this…

This was suddenly an overwhelming need. He stooped to pull Emma's hands from her face, he saw the despair etched deep in her eyes, he saw the lingering horror, and he saw the shuddering sobs rack her body—he couldn't bear it. He took her in his arms. When she slumped against him, helpless in the face of her grief and shock and exhaustion, he simply lifted her up and cradled her against him and rocked her as if she were a child.

He held her while the shuddering sobs went on and on. He simply held her.

From inside the door Kyle's father caught his eye over Emma's dark curls, and he came to the door of his son's room.

'Take care of her,' he said to Dev. 'I dunno how to thank her. Thank her from me. Thank her from us.'

Then he gently closed the door to his son's room and Dev was left alone in the deserted corridor. With Emma.

She was past coherent thought, he decided. Past coherent action. Her face was in his shoulder and he could feel her tears soaking through the fabric of his shirt. She was moulding her body against him. The heat of her body was warming him and he felt...he felt...

No. This was crazy. He didn't feel anything.

She was a patient in trouble. A colleague in trouble who'd collapsed. Nothing more.

She smelled like rose water and—sump oil?

It was a heady combination.

It shouldn't make him feel like... Like what? He didn't know. All he knew was that holding her filled a need in him as well as a need in her. He was taking comfort as well as giving it.

The shuddering eased a little. His face was in her hair.

'Hush,' he told her.

He kissed the dusty crop of deep black curls, as one would have kissed a child. 'Hush.'

It might not be professional but he needed to do it. His arms were cradling her as if she was the most precious thing.

What she'd done that day...

What to do now?

Somehow he had to switch back to being a doctor. Somehow.

The room next door was empty. He pushed the door wide with his foot and strode in. He needed to lay her on the bed, call for Margaret, examine her...

But for a long moment he did nothing. He simply stood, cradling her, whispering into her soft dark curls, giving warmth, taking warmth.

And finally, finally the sobs subsided. She seemed to realise where she was, what she was doing. She pulled away—just a little—though her arms were still around his neck and her breasts were still soft against his chest. Her eyes widened as she looked into his face, seeming to realise for the first time that she was in a strange man's arms.

But here was no alarm. Her body was limp, as if she'd gone past the point where she cared what was happening.

'I'm sorry.'

'Don't be.'

'I don't cry,' she said.

'I can see that. I guess it must have been raining on my shoulder.'

She attempted a chuckle, but it came out ragged, as if she wasn't sure where to begin to pick up the pieces of sanity.

'I... If you'll put me down...'

'You'll fall over.'

'I will not.' The strength was returning to her voice. A little.

'How about if I put you on the bed?'

'I don't need to be put on the bed.'

'You do, you know,' he said seriously. 'You copped a fair whack on your head this morning, and you've been crawling through a bus full of broken glass. You need to be checked. How pregnant are you?'

'Seven months. I'm fine.'

'You're not. Apart from checking your baby, I can see at least three nasty scratches that need cleaning.'

'I don't need—'

'Your baby needs to be checked,' he said inexorably. 'You know that's right. You have medical training. Pregnant woman. Car crash. Trauma. Check the baby.'

She stilled in his hold. He had a valid point and he could see her acknowledging it.

'I'm right, aren't I?' He was smiling—just a little. Regardless of the trauma and the horror of the day, there was something about this woman that made him want to smile. She'd said she never cried. He could believe it. Something about her said that she was built for loving and laughing. Something told him that Emma—whoever Emma was—usually met life head on and greeted it with unfeigned pleasure.

There was laughter in her face—subdued now, but ready to spring back at any moment. She had real courage.

And she had sense.

'OK. Maybe you're right,' she said—grudgingly. 'So my baby needs to be checked. Do you have an obstetrician on call? A female obstetrician?'

'This is a small hospital. There's me. Or there's me. Or, again, there's me.'

'Then I'll check myself, thank you very much.'

'You can't.'

'Lend me a stethoscope. You might have figured by now that I'm a doctor. I can check my baby's heartbeat just as well as you can. And as for my nether regions…not in a million years, Dr O'Halloran.'

'You need—'

'You can check my scratches and my bumped head,' she told him, with such graciousness that he smiled.

'Gee, thanks.'

'You ought to be grateful. It's not everyone who gets to check the inside of my left elbow, which is where I have my deepest scratch. Now, will you put me down? I'm not in the habit of lying in my doctor's arms when I'm about to have my left elbow examined.'

She was trying for laughter. After all that had gone on that day, she was trying to make him smile.

He was stunned. He stared down into her tear-stained face and he could hardly believe that she was trying for laughter.

She had such courage.

'I'm honoured,' he told her, in a voice that he couldn't quite make steady. He made to put her down on the coverlet but she held on for just a fraction of a second more than she needed to.

'Um…'

He paused. 'Um?'

'Dr O'Halloran?'

'Yes?'

Her laughter had faded. A little. Her face was suddenly serious.

'Thank you for holding me,' she said, in a voice that matched his for uncertainty. 'I… My need for that has been a long time coming and hopefully it'll never come again—but thank you for being here for me.'

She closed her eyes for a millisecond and when she opened them something had changed. She'd withdrawn, just a little. She was somehow…back under control? There was laughter back in her eyes but something told him that it was a shield. A shield from what? He didn't know.

'OK,' she said, businesslike now. Moving on. 'Let's get these scratches seen to. Let's forget you ever saw me being a wimp.'

'Yes, ma'am.'

It was almost peaceful, Emma decided.

She was dressed now in a hospital gown—a very fetching shade of faded green—and Dev and

Margaret were systematically taking care of her damage.

Margaret had bustled in when Dev had rung the bell. She'd shooed Dev out. She and a junior nurse had helped Emma change, washing her and tutting over her as if she were a child. Then Margaret had called Dev back.

Now Dev was cleaning slivers of glass from the myriad scratches Emma had collected in the smashed bus, while Margaret assisted. There was nothing Emma could do but lie there while they fussed. All she could do was lie back and let them be in control.

For now she didn't have to think about anything. She couldn't.

Soon it would all crowd back, she knew. There were complications here—lots of complications— but she didn't have room in her jumbled consciousness to figure them out.

So she lay back and let her head sink into the pillows. She let her mind drift and she let Dev do as he willed.

'She's gone to sleep.' It was Margaret. She was a good nurse, Emma thought inconsequentially, without opening her eyes. Rigid, though. A go-by-the-rules sort.

'She deserves to sleep,' Dev was saying. 'It's been a hell of an introduction to the town.'

'Why is she here?' Margaret was adjusting a dressing on her knee. It was surreal, Emma thought from her haze of semi-sleep. She was floating. They could do what they willed—say what they willed—she didn't care. She was beyond caring.

'I have no idea,' Dev replied. 'Do we know who she is? Apart from the fact that her name's Emma?'

'I thought you'd have asked her.' Margaret seemed startled. 'You decided to admit her.'

'I picked her up in the corridor and carried her in here. That's hardly admitting her.'

Margaret sounded shocked. 'So we don't have any admission forms. We don't even have any identity. Dev, for heaven's sake…'

'Hey, Margaret, she's hardly likely to sue.'

'But if she haemorrhages… If she dies on us…'

Hey! That wasn't a good thought. Emma let it drift and found it vaguely troubling. But not too troubling. She figured she should open her eyes and rebut the likelihood of haemorrhaging—and then she figured it was all too much trouble. Haemorrhage, haemorrhage. Who cared?

Someone was pulling the covers up now. It had to be Dev. His big hand were tucking the sheets around her, lingering just a little—almost as a blessing.

She liked his hands.

He smelt nice.

Nope. She wasn't going to die. Not when she had her head on these pillows and this man was tucking her in and she was safe.

'I guess we need to find out.' He sounded almost reluctant.

'Her handbag's here,' Margaret was saying. 'Helen brought it in. Someone found it in her car and put it in the ambulance. You want me to look?'

'We know she's Emma. We know she's a doctor.'

'We need a full name for the records,' Margaret told him. 'If you think she can sleep here when I don't have a name…'

Would they throw her out of the hospital if she didn't have a name? Emma thought inconsequentially. Surely not.

Damn, she should open her eyes. She should.

She didn't.

'I'm looking,' Margaret said.

OK. She had to face this some time. Complications…

Wake up, Emma, she told herself. Wake up and face the music.

'There's no need,' she said, with as much dignity as a three-quarters asleep and very pregnant doctor in a too scant hospital gown could muster. 'I'm Emma O'Halloran. I'm Dr O'Halloran, just the same as Dev. Just the same—but different.'

She struggled for something else to say but nothing else occurred to her. 'Now, if you don't mind, I need to go to sleep. Goodnight.'

If they thought any more explanations were possible today, they had another think coming.

Dr Emma O'Halloran had reached the end.

Emma might sleep. Dev couldn't.

First there was the work. The traumatised kids from the morning had to be seen, one by one, talking them through the event with care. Some time tomorrow he'd welcome a team of qualified counsellors from the city, to take care of these kids as they must be cared for if there weren't to be long-term psychological problems, but for now Dev was all they had.

He saw the worst cases. He should see them all, but the night beat him. Parents took their kids home and coped as best they could, and Dev could only hope that cuddles and their own beds were the best medicine.

But one kid he had to talk to. One little girl whose courage shone like a beacon. He rang Katy's parents and asked to speak to her in person.

'Suzy's going to be OK,' he told her. 'She's already in Brisbane and the doctors there say she'll be fine. Jodie will be fine, too. And the doctors down in Brisbane are also telling me that you saved Mr Jeffries's life. You did a wonderful job today, Katy, and we'll never forget it.'

There was a silence followed by the sound of sobbing, and Katy's dad came on the phone.

'I think she'll be OK,' her dad said. 'Her mum's got her wrapped in warm blankets by the stove and she's been cuddled since we got her home.'

'Hug her from me,' he told the man. 'You have a kid in a million.'

He smiled as he replaced the phone. Katy was the runt of the litter—an afterthought in a family of rough boys. She'd given the town a gift today, he thought, but he'd see she personally got one in return. There wasn't a better kid to hold the mantle of heroine.

That was his last urgent case.

It was after ten. He hesitated—then walked back through the hospital wards and opened the door on his patient. On Emma O'Halloran. She was still soundly asleep.

'She woke and ate a little supper,' Janelle, the night charge nurse, told him, coming into the room behind him. 'But she went straight back to sleep. She said she was a bit sore but her headache has eased.'

Good. That meant he could relax. Right?

How the hell could he relax?

Things were still jarring, and one thing jarred most of all. O'Halloran. She'd said her name was O'Halloran.

And when Emma had first opened her eyes—way back at the crash scene—she'd called him Corey.

The two facts merged into a blur of unreality.

Surely not.

And then there was the way he felt about her. Or the way he didn't know how he felt about her. She'd sobbed on his shoulder and he, a man who hated tears, who steered clear of emotion at all costs, had wanted to stay holding her...

This was crazy. Get on with it. Sort out facts.

He drove home—the two miles out of town to the rambling doctor's residence by Stony Creek. It was a great old house, built where the creek met the sea. It held such memories. This house had raised them. His father had been the GP here, and his father before him. Corey and Dev had argued endlessly when they'd been kids about who would have this house.

In the end no one had wanted it.

Since Corey's illness, the house had seemed hollow, and when Corey had died, his mother had moved out. She'd bought a new little brick unit in town. Ostensibly it had been so that Dev could be independent, but in reality it was because she was haunted by Corey. Corey's laughter. Corey's life.

His father's death had been gentle, a natural death at the end of a long life, and his memory seemed a peaceful blessing. But not Corey's.

He himself should move out himself, Dev thought. He didn't like coming home to this house.

But it was a great house.

For a family?

Yeah, right. How would he grow a family?

With Margaret?

And hell, there was another complication, he thought savagely. How had that happened? It had sort of sneaked up on him when he'd been too busy to notice, and he didn't have a clue what to do about it.

He couldn't think of that tonight. He wanted solitude, but that wasn't going to happen.

Sure enough, his mother was waiting for him—as always. Lorna had not only moved out of the family house since Corey's death—she'd also edged herself away from local friends. She was desperately lonely. Every night she cooked a meal for him, for which he was grateful, and she needed to talk—for which he wasn't so grateful.

Not tonight. He wanted bed. He wanted space.

But somehow he managed to haul himself together and talk through the day's events. Matter-of-factly. Trying not to let the emotion of the day enter his voice.

He needn't have worried. The tragedy of Kyle's death barely seemed to touch her, which was a measure of how distant and depressed she'd been since her own son's death.

But, surprisingly, she was interested in Emma. He didn't tell her about the O'Halloran connection but it seemed she had a connection of her own.

'You don't suppose this lady doctor might have been my visitor?' she said slowly, almost as if she was afraid. 'I've been thinking... Maybe she was. Because no one came and I'd made lunch specially.' She managed a wan smile. 'That was why you got this casserole tonight. I made beef stroganoff specially.'

He wasn't listing to the beef stroganoff bit. 'What do you mean—your visitor?'

'I told you.' She sighed. 'At least, I think I told you. I was expecting someone for lunch.'

His heart seemed to skip a beat and when it started again things weren't normal. He paused, tightening, waiting for he didn't know what.

Hardly daring to ask.

But he had to ask. 'Who were you expecting?'

'A friend of Corey's.' She seemed to have lost interest again. She'd packed her empty casserole dish into a wicker basket and now she was adjusting a cloth to protect what was left inside. 'At least that's who she said she was. A woman rang me from Brisbane last night and she asked if it was OK to come up and see me. I... I said of course. I didn't say I didn't know he had friends. She said her name was Emma and she'd known Corey years ago. But then...I waited and she never came.'

'The doctor I told you about,' he said slowly, his mind racing. 'Her name is Emma.'

Her mother looked at him then, her face almost pleading. 'Do you think...? Could she really be a friend of Corey's?'

'I'll ask her.'

Corey was dead.

With all the events of the day there was no way he should be thinking of his brother tonight. But he was.

He lay and stared up at the ceiling and thought of his younger brother. As he remembered him. As he'd loved him.

Emma O'Halloran.

Coincidence? Or not?

Not, he thought heavily. He thought of the way she'd opened her eyes that morning and looked up to him. And the way she'd said his brother's name.

No, he thought.

Not coincidence.

CHAPTER FOUR

HE WAS there again when Emma woke. She opened her eyes and he was smiling down at her and he was…there.

'Corey?'

'Corey's my brother.'

She blinked.

Not Corey. Of course not. How could she have thought that?

Dev.

He was sitting on her bedside chair. The morning sun was streaming in over her coverlet.

She was in hospital.

The events of yesterday flooded back. Reality.

She jerked up in bed and stared around wildly. She was in a single ward in hospital. She had dressings on her arms. She was wearing a hospital gown.

Dev was sitting beside her. He was holding her wrist.

Dev. Not Corey. Definitely not Corey. Corey had never made her feel like…

Whoa. Cut it out.

She glanced at the bedside clock. Eight a.m. No! She snatched back her wrist from Dev as if his touch burned.

'Where are my clothes?' It wasn't the politest of greetings but it was all she could think of. She had to get out of here. Fast.

'In the hospital laundry,' he told her.

'My suitcase?'

'Smashed in the accident.' His eyes didn't leave her face. 'I'm sorry, but the tow-truck driver said that most of your clothes have been damaged. The case was thrown out and...' He gave a rueful smile. 'One of the emergency service vehicles seems to have driven over it. But Madge says you're not to worry. Madge—our tow-truck driver—reckons you're about her size and she's been pregnant four times so she knows what's comfortable. She's volunteered to find you something as soon as the shops open.'

'When the shops open?' She was having trouble taking this in. Someone had driven over her suitcase. A tow-truck driver called Madge was shopping for her.

It didn't make sense.

It didn't matter. Move on, she told herself. Get practical. Fast. 'When will the shops open?'

He glanced at his watch. 'In about an hour.'

She thought about that. 'Can you, please, tell Madge that my need is urgent? Tell her I'm deeply appreciative but I need help fast. And…where can I hire a car?'

'You can't.' He smiled down at her, a slow, reassuring smile that was so unlike Corey's that she almost gasped. It was a chameleon effect—one minute he was like Corey, the next he was just…Dev.

'What's the urgency?' he asked.

Smile or not, she needed to concentrate on priorities. 'I need to catch a plane.'

'An overseas flight?'

'Yes.'

'You're English?'

'Yes.'

'You'd have to be,' he said slowly. 'If you loved Corey.'

Silence.

Why had she ever come here? she wondered, confusion and horror, mingling. How was she to get back to Brisbane in time for her flight? It was stupid. Stupid!

She'd left travelling here until the last minute. She'd put it off and put it off. Then she'd thought she must—how much easier to explain when there wasn't a baby to complicate flights, complicate emotions. But now—it all seemed stupid.

And if she didn't catch the plane…

She had to catch the plane.

'My flight leaves Brisbane at four this afternoon,' she told him. 'I have to be on it. I need to hire a car. Please.'

He lifted her wrist again and took her pulse slowly, refusing to be hurried. 'You can't catch a plane this afternoon.'

'I must.' She was pulling back on her wrist. She didn't like him touching her. Or maybe she did. He made her feel… He made her feel…

She didn't know how he made her feel. But the sensation of his touch certainly wasn't helping her confusion. 'I'm fine,' she managed.

'Did you know that you bled in the night?'

She stopped pulling away, and froze. 'I bled?'

'Janelle didn't think you were awake enough to take it in.' Then, as he saw the panic surge in her eyes, he moved swiftly to reassure her. 'It wasn't a major bleed. Spotting. It's not surprising, the way your little one was thrown about yesterday. If you rest, it should settle. It probably already has. There's been nothing since two a.m. But you need to rest.'

She stared up at him, appalled.

'I spotted?'

'Yes.'

'I can't lose my baby.' It was a terrified whisper—and there came that smile again. It was a killer smile. It warmed…places that desperately needed to be warmed.

It made the fear recede a little. If he smiled like that…

No. Doctors didn't necessarily make it better. Who'd know that better than she?

'We have an obstetrician coming here this morning,' he told her with the air of someone pulling a rabbit out of a hat. 'Harriet Straw visits once a week to see our expectant mums.' His smile widened. 'You'll be pleased to know that she's even a female.' Then, as her look of horror didn't fade, he sat again and took her hand in his.

'Harriet's good, Emma. She's old-fashioned and she's thorough. I want her to give you a really thorough examination and I trust her judgement absolutely. If she says you need to be moved to a Brisbane hospital, we'll do it. But I'm thinking now that she'll say bed rest for a few days should see you right. But I'm also guessing she'll say no flying.'

She gulped. She glanced at the bedside clock. She glanced at her bulge.

'I can't go until I'm examined?' she whispered.

'You know you can't.'

She did. Damnably she did.

She had to catch the plane.

Not if it meant endangering her baby.

He was watching her face, reading the conflicting emotions washing over her features. She could see that he was almost as confused as she was.

'You really are a doctor?' he asked.

'No.' She was preoccupied with far more important thoughts than whether she was a doctor, and surely he had the sense to see it. 'I learned my tracheostomy skills at an adult education hobby class—right along with brain surgery for beginners.'

He smiled, rueful. 'I'm sorry.'

'So am I. If I miss that flight… Do you realise how pregnant I am?'

'You told me that you were seven months.'

'That's right. Twenty-eight weeks, to be precise.'

He frowned, thinking it through. Seeing where she was coming from. 'Twenty-eight weeks. Isn't that the limit for international flying?'

'Yes,' she said, in the tone of one speaking to someone with the brains of a very small newt. 'I can't fly after twenty-eight weeks. That's the rule for nearly every international airline. I'm big for my dates and they made the biggest fuss when I booked. I only managed it by getting a doctor's certificate saying the examining doctors were sure things were OK and I didn't look like delivering early.'

He frowned. 'You won't get those certificates now.'

'No.' Her voice was practically a wail. 'Thanks to you.'

'Hey,' he said, startled. 'What did I have to do with it?'

'You put me to bed.'

'If I hadn't, you'd have fallen over.'

She glowered.

'It's not my fault,' he said more mildly, and she glowered some more.

'So you can stop glowering.'

She thought about it. 'Glowering helps,' she told him. 'What else can I do but glower?'

He grinned. 'Maybe you can hire a ship,' he said, helpfully, and the glower intensified.

He chuckled. Just a bit. But then his laughter died. As did hers. There was nothing funny about her situation and they both knew it.

'I'm sorry, but you are stuck,' he told her. 'You've lost a little blood. The bleeding's stopped but I'm sure that Harriet will insist on a few days' bed rest. She's not going to let you fly. So you need to move on to plan B. Do you have friends in Australia—a place where you can stay until the baby's born?'

'No.'

'When did you come to Australia?'

'The day before yesterday.'

His face stilled. 'The day before yesterday.'

'Yes.'

'So I'm right,' he said slowly. 'You were my mother's visitor who never came. You came because of Corey.'

'Y-yes.'

'And your name. O'Halloran?' The question seemed to come reluctantly. Very reluctantly. 'Is that because of Corey as well?'

She stared up into his face. How was she going to say this?

Back in England, saying it had seemed dreadful. She'd tried to write. She'd tried to phone. But every time the words simply wouldn't come.

Finally she'd walked into a travel agent and booked a ticket, telling herself that if she flew halfway round the world, the words would have to come. She'd look at Corey's family and she'd see their reaction and she'd be able to break it slowly, or...or something.

In truth it had been a dumb plan, she told herself. Dumb, dumb, dumb.

How much dumber now?

'So you came to see my mother,' Dev said softly. And waited.

Outside a plover was calling a warning, guarding his nest, calling over and over. She wanted to be outside with the plover, she thought. She didn't want to be here, with this man, telling him what she must.

'I was married to Corey,' she whispered. 'I'm Emma O'Halloran. I'm your brother's widow.'

The silence went on and on. It stretched out for so long it became a void, sucking everything into it.

Corey was with them. Corey, with his wonderful smile, with his magnetic laughter. With his madness.

'When did you marry Corey?' Dev asked at last, as if the words were dragged out of him.

'Three years ago.'

'Three…'

'He was almost well,' she whispered. 'Almost. I thought he was.'

'Will you tell me?' She'd distressed him, she thought. Of course she had. Every word seemed to be dragged out of him.

Well, what had she expected? This was why she hadn't come for so long. If it hadn't been for the baby, she wouldn't be here now.

He had to know. She had to tell him.

'I was working for Médecins Sans Frontières,' she told him. 'In Ethopia. I'd always told myself I'd work for them for a while, as soon as I qualified. I'd spend a couple of years trying to…make a difference.'

'It's a fantastic organisation,' Dev said softly. 'Sending doctors anywhere in the world where there's desperate need.'

'There's always desperate need. They're always short of doctors.' Her voice was bleak. She knew it was but she didn't know how to change it. 'We had doctors from all around the world working with us. But…it was awful work. You can't do it for ever. You burn out. I spent two years working with famine-affected kids and it beat me. At the end I was emotionally and physically exhausted. Physically at the end. And then Corey arrived.'

'Corey.' His voice was a wondering whisper.

'Corey was…a little bit of magic,' she told him, biting her lip and trying to remember that time. Trying to remember the joy. 'He arrived unannounced, and he worked like he was unstoppable. His need for work was insatiable. He went from patient to patient, working his magic. And he laughed. He was on a constant high. In that dreadful place he was like a beacon of hope. He made the children smile. Tiny malnourished children who had no hope at all…he made them smile. He brought laughter into that dreadful place and it was such a gift.' She paused and then she smiled, remembering. 'It was a gift to me.'

'So you fell in love.' There was still wonder in his voice and she looked up at him and she smiled some more. This was a good memory to share. One of the very few.

'Of course I fell in love,' she whispered. 'At least, I thought I did. I thought I knew him. We were married by the camp chaplain and it was a wonderful, magic thing to do. We had a party—with only our rice rations and water but it still felt great. It was the best time.'

'And then you discovered he was sick?'

'We came back to Britain,' she told him. 'I'd been ill. I don't think... Maybe I wasn't seeing straight even before I met Corey. Anyway, I couldn't cope any more, not even with Corey's magic. So he said he'd bring me home to England.'

'You didn't discuss coming to Australia? To meet his family?' Dev's face was closed. She couldn't see what he was thinking. She could only guess.

'As I said, I was ill—too ill to travel anywhere but home—and Corey said he had no family.' Then, as she saw a wave of pain wash over Dev's face, she closed her eyes and lay back on the pillows. She'd been so hurt, but so must this man have been. Dev and his family.

But she needed to explain. Explain why she hadn't seen the demons behind Corey's magic.

'I...I'd been so ill,' she whispered. 'I'd been fighting dysentery for months. I'd had malaria and I was at the end of my resources. If I'd met Corey at any other time I probably would have pushed to know more of his background. Maybe I would have realised...'

'That he was manic?'

'Yes.' She hated saying it—but she had to. 'He was so ill. He was on medication I never knew about. But he was on such a high. The medicine, our marriage, bringing me home to England…it must have made him feel that he no longer needed his medication. And when he crashed… I was just appalled. I finally realised how his energy levels had been maintained. I finally realised how sick he was.'

She paused, hating to see the look of pain on Dev's face. Hating to tell him what she needed to. 'I don't even know… To this day I don't know how sick he was,' she admitted. 'How long he'd been sick. I just don't know.'

'He was diagnosed at university,' Dev told her. 'Manic depression. He'd been on medication since he was twenty.'

'I'd guessed he must have been,' she told him. 'It was all so obvious when I knew.' She paused again but Dev lifted her hand and pressed it, compelling her to go on.

'And then what happened?' he asked, and the caring in his tone was almost her undoing. But she'd sobbed already on this man's shoulder. There was no way she was doing it again.

'As soon as I was well enough, I tried to talk to him,' she said. 'He'd been erratic, making me guess there was a problem. I'd been admitted to hospital but he was only visiting me spasmodi-cally. The last time I saw him I asked him straight out what was happening. I asked him…' She bit her lip. 'I asked him straight out to tell me what medication he should be on.'

'He'd hate that.'

'He did,' she said wearily. 'So much that as soon as I asked the question, he didn't want to know me.'

'Emma…!'

It was a protest. She glanced at his face—and closed her eyes again. She didn't want to know. She had enough of her own pain. She couldn't af-ford to get sucked into his.

'I was too ill to do much,' she told him. 'I tried…to stay in touch. He got a job up in Scotland and I tried to contact him. But he just drove me away. He wouldn't let me near.'

'Like he did us.'

'I guessed,' she told him. 'By then I'd thought that he probably had a family back here who might even care, but there was nothing I could do. He wouldn't talk about you. The last time—the second-last time—I talked to him, by phone, he said he was fine again and he'd decided he'd go back to Ethiopia. He said he'd just come to England because of me but now… He said by find-ing out that he was ill I'd destroyed our marriage.

That was what he said. He said he couldn't bear me knowing. And that was...that was the end.'

'I'm so sorry.'

'There's no reason for you to be sorry for me,' she told him, trying for some asperity. 'You have your own problems.' Her voice settled. She'd done the hardest bit. Or almost the hardest bit. 'It was a strange time,' she told him. 'The time in Ethopia. I was lonely and unhappy and driven, and in a way I think Corey saved my life. He surely saved my sanity. You know, I'm holding onto that. I can't help Corey any more, but he knew how much he'd done for me, and in some strange way that helps me.'

He nodded, grave, and she thought, He understands. It was a good feeling. A solid feeling.

This man must understand, she thought, and once more there was this tug of something she didn't understand. This...connection.

It'd be because of Corey, she told herself. What else could it be?

'So that's the last you saw of him?' Dev asked, and she dragged herself back to the past. Back to Corey.

'No.'

He stilled. 'No?'

'Not quite. I didn't see him for over two years. I'd even started to get on with my life.'

'But you didn't divorce him?'

'No.'

'So when did you see him last?' Dev's voice was flat, uninflectioned, and Emma looked at him. Really looked at him. He'd loved his brother, she thought. All these years she'd wondered what Corey's family would be like, and now she knew. Corey's family. Her baby's family.

Dev.

It seemed right. More than right.

'Seven months back,' she whispered. 'I know that. I saw him…the night before he died.'

His face froze.

'You saw him?'

'He came to my hospital apartment.' This was the worst. She could hardly bear to say it. 'I'd just come off duty. It was my birthday and I was happy. The paediatric team had given me a little party and all my patients had sung 'Happy Birthday' and we'd had a cake. I came back to my apartment carrying the biggest bunch of tulips—and Corey was there.'

Silence. There were two trains of thought here, running at a tangent to each other.

'We hadn't seen him for years either,' Dev said slowly. 'After Ethiopia we lost touch. I knew he was worse. I was trying to find him. I was trying desperately to find him.'

'He was dreadful,' she whispered. There was no way to dress this up. It had to be told like it was.

'Just…despairing. He hadn't eaten. He was thin to the point of emaciation. He came in and I cradled him and I bathed him and fed him and…and I just held him. I knew he needed medical help badly, but that night holding him seemed the only thing I could do. So I just held him. Then, at some time in the small hours, I must have fallen asleep, and when I woke up he was gone.'

Dev flinched. As if struck. 'When was this?'

'September. September ten.'

'The day before he suicided.'

'I didn't know,' she said bleakly. 'I started making enquiries. And then I heard. He'd fallen under a train. That night.'

'You held him the night he died?'

'Yes.'

'Dear God,' Dev said, and put his face in his hands.

'And then you were there,' Emma whispered. 'Or members of your family. He'd gone north, caught the train north before…before it ended, and by the time I found out, the authorities must have located you. I contacted the police and they said his family from Australia were already there. You'd come to claim him. And then it didn't seem right. To jump in on your grief and say here I am, his wife of a few weeks two years ago; his wife who hadn't seen him for two years; his wife who hadn't been able to help him one bit.'

There was a long, long silence. Heavy. There was grief here that had been unsaid for these long months, Emma thought bleakly. For these long years.

There was still one unanswered question that had to be asked, and Dev asked it now, slowly, as if he wasn't sure he had the right to know that answer.

'The baby…'

'This baby is Corey's,' she said, and her eyes met his, unflinching. 'I didn't know…I never dreamed… But, of course, that night when he needed me so much, the last thing I thought of was birth control. Then, when he was dead, I didn't think past his loss. So I was three months pregnant before I guessed.'

Once more there was a silence. 'If you'd known earlier,' he said heavily, as if it was a question to which he hardly wanted the answer, 'would you have got rid of it?'

There was a stunned pause.

'You have to be kidding.' Her eyes blazed with anger at that. 'No.' She shook her head, fierce in the face of one of the few things in her life that remained an inviolate truth. 'Corey and I…well, it was a mess. We met when we were both ill. We needed each other and we clung and we married when maybe we were stupid to do so. But at the time…I thought I loved Corey. I know, he was too ill to love me back for long, in any way that was meaningful, and I was too ill to know him any more than superficially. But I loved the glimpses of him that I had, the Corey he was under the dreadfulness, and if there's anything good to come of all this mess, it's that I'm carrying his child. I don't know whether it was the right thing or the wrong thing to come all this way to tell you this— to lay this knowledge on you. But Corey will live on in his child. And maybe…maybe you need to know.' Her voice faltered. 'You need to know.'

Once more she looked into his face. It was a strong face, she thought. Strong in a way Corey's never was. There were traces of pain, life lines etched under the laughter. Being Corey's brother could never have been easy.

'Can you afford to take care of a baby on your own?' he asked, and she dragged herself back to their discussion.

'Of course I can.' She flinched. 'Are you thinking I came all this way to ask for financial help?'

'I didn't think anything of the sort,' he said gently, wonderingly. He shook his head as if he could hardly believe what he was hearing. 'You came into my life as a heroine, Emma O'Halloran. There's been nothing said in the last ten minutes that's dispelled that impression. My belief in your heroism still stands.'

She flushed. 'I'm no heroine.'

'No.' He stood. 'Maybe you're not. Maybe you're just Emma. Emma who held my brother the night he died. And Emma who's come halfway around the world to give her child the right to meet his father's family. To give us that gift.'

'It's no gift.'

'It is a gift, Emma,' he told her in a voice that was none too steady. He took a deep breath and appeared to regroup. 'Emma, you need to sleep. I'm sorry you're missing your flight.' Then, as if he'd just heard what he'd said and reconsidered, he shook his head. 'No. I'm not sorry. It's given you grave problems and they need to be sorted. But that can be sorted. Meanwhile, I'm asking that you don't worry. That you put yourself in my hands for a while and let yourself be cared for. See Harriet, get your baby checked, let Madge buy you a few frilly nighties and…' He hesitated. 'And let my mother come to visit you?'

'Your mother?'

'Lorna. Dad died two years ago. There's only my mother. But…' He smiled suddenly, a wide smile that had all the joy of the morning behind it. 'My mother thought my brother died alone. That he'd seen no one and that no one cared. That he made the choice to die because he was alone. But you held him. You cradled him. You've given her—us—the greatest gift. And now you're telling me that you're carrying her grandson. She'll love to see you, Emma. She'll love you to bits. We…we both will.'

And before she knew what he was about, he bent and kissed her.

It was supposed to be a feather-light kiss, a kiss of gratitude. A kiss of a brother-in-law acknowledging for the first time that his brother had had a wife. That was what she expected.

It was no such thing.

Sure, it was a brush of lips against her forehead. Only that.

But the feel of it…the feel of him…

He backed away, as if the shock of it had hit him, too, leaving him confused. It wasn't what was meant to happen.

Somehow he managed a smile, albeit a shaky one.

'Sleep, Emma,' he whispered, as her fingers came up to touch the place where his lips had touched. 'Sleep.'

He walked out the door without another word—and she lay against the pillows and held her fingers against her forehead. For a very long time.

It made a difference.

Last night he'd held her and things had somehow…changed.

She was Corey's widow.

It made a difference.

*   *   *

Dr Harriet Straw was blunt to the point of rudeness, but incredibly reassuring.

'Given the fact that you were thrown out of the car—they're telling me the seat-belt moorings were smashed—there's every reason to expect a little bleeding. I would have expected a lot of bleeding. You're covered with external bruising. You'll have internal bruises as well, but the fact that you've only had a tiny amount of spotting and the baby has a heart beat that's stronger than mine…well, you've been damned lucky, girl.'

'Does that mean that I can—?'

'It does not mean you can fly. It doesn't mean you can get out of this bed. Let's assume there's a tiny tear somewhere. You put pressure on it before it has a chance to heal and it'll get bigger. You need three days in bed, followed by two weeks without lifting or carrying. In fact, given your due date, no lifting or carrying until after the birth—and definitely no flying. Air pressure does all sorts of funny things to blood vessels at the best of times.'

'I can't stay here until after the birth.' She flinched. 'I can't.'

There was a tap on the door. Harriet tugged it open and Dev was there. She nodded to him and then went right on.

'I can organise emergency accommodation down in Brisbane,' she told her. 'But not until that three days is up.' She glanced cursorily at Dev. 'The baby's fine,' she told him. 'But Emma stays put. There's emergency accommodation units attached to Brisbane Hospital where she can stay once she's safe to move.'

'That won't be necessary,' Dev told them. 'If Emma doesn't have friends or family in Australia, she can stay here.'

'In this town?' Harriet frowned. 'The school holidays start next week and you know what that means. The place is booked out twelve months ahead. Since when did you have emergency accommodation?'

'I mean she can stay at our place.'

'What…?'

'This is Corey's baby,' Dev told her, and Harriet stared.

Harriet was a plump little woman in her sixties. Owlish. She had a mop of white curls tied up in an unruly bun and the curls were escaping all around her face. Now she stared at Dev, took her glasses off, stared some more, wiped her glasses and then put them back on.

'Corey's baby,' she muttered.

'Yes.'

'You didn't tell me that.' She glared at Dev and then turned to glare down at Emma. 'You didn't tell me.'

'We're telling you now,' Dev said.

Harriet stared down at Emma as if she'd suddenly grown two heads. 'You're carrying my godson's baby?'

'If your godson was Corey then I guess I am,' Emma told her.

Harriet swallowed.

'Does Lorna know?' she demanded.

'I'll tell her now,' Dev said.

Harriet swallowed again.

And then she burst into tears.

CHAPTER FIVE

THAT was just only the start of it. It was just as well she'd been ordered to stay in bed. There was so much swirling in Emma's mind that, for the next few days, to do anything else but lie back on the pillows and think about what she was facing in the future was beyond her.

She had a family.

No. Her baby had a family.

It was astounding.

Emma was an only child of elderly parents. Her father had died when she'd been only ten. Her mother was concerned to do the right thing, but her emotional attachment was almost non-existent. This emotion was just plain astonishing.

She'd expected…well, she hadn't known what she'd expected. She'd decided it was the right thing to tell Corey's family that she was having his child, but for them to embrace the idea with so much…so much…

So much love, she thought as she lay back on her pillows and let it sink in. There was no other way of describing it.

After Harriet's outburst, Dev and Harriet had left her, but they hadn't gone far before Harriet's need to talk had overcome her. Emma had therefore overheard them talking urgently in the corridor outside her room.

'Tell your mother straight away, Dev.'

'I'll tell her tonight.'

'No. You get home right away and tell her now. Lorna deserves to know this minute and if you don't go and tell her right now, I will.'

'I don't know how she'll take it.'

'Well, I do.' They hadn't shut the door completely, and they'd been oblivious of the fact that Emma had still been able to hear them. 'Your mother has never forgiven herself that no one was there for Corey. That he had a wife…and now a baby… Oh, Dev, it'll make such a difference.' Emma had heard an unmistakable sniff from the businesslike little obstetrician and then the sounds of decision. 'Come on, boy. We'll tell her together. Right now.'

They had. Then, half an hour later, Lorna O'Halloran had appeared at the ward door. She'd been weeping—and any doubt Emma had had as to whether she'd done the right thing in travelling to the other side of the world to meet Corey's family had been banished right then.

It made Emma acknowledge even more fully that manic depression was an insidious physical disease. She thought it through as she lay back in her bed over the following few days, letting her body heal and her thoughts drift where they would. There was no way Corey's mental state had been caused by problems in his past. Corey had been loved to bits by his family. By his mother, by his father and by his older brother.

By Dev.

Dev…

She was thinking about him now—and as if by magic he appeared at her door. He'd been popping in intermittently since she'd been admitted, checking her obs, reassuring her, smiling at her…

That was part of the reason she was confused, she decided. He just had to smile at her and she was confused all over again.

It was because he was like Corey, she told herself. It had to be. There was no reason for her to be so darned confused.

But he was standing in the doorway now and he was smiling and she was confused all over again.

Not because of Corey.

'Awake?'

Drat that smile. It had no business to do what it did. 'I'm awake.' She struggled to rise and he was right by her side, finding another pillow, helping her.

He was far too close.

He was far too confusing.

'Of course I'm awake,' she managed, and was annoyed that her voice sounded a bit breathless. 'I'm so awake I'm bored.'

'Really?'

'Really.'

He smiled again. Did he realise what effect he had on her? She wished he'd stop it.

No. She didn't wish he'd stop.

'Then maybe it's time we talked about the next few months,' he said, and her odd sense of unreality receded.

'Maybe we shouldn't.'

'You need to think about it. You've slept for four days.'

'I have not!'

'Give or take an hour or two. Your body really did receive a battering.'

'I'm fine.'

'You're better now,' he said gently. 'You're still not fine. But that's beside the point. I talked to Harriet this afternoon and she says I can take you home tomorrow.'

'Home.' She stared at him. 'You know where my home is. London, England. Unless you have an ocean liner tied up at the local wharf, it's not going to happen.'

He smiled again but shook his head. 'Maybe you need to redefine home. For the moment.' He hesitated. 'Margaret tells me you've been on the phone to England. You've let everyone know what's happening?'

'Everyone? Yeah.'

'Do you have family?'

'I have a boyfriend,' she said stiffly.

'A boyfriend?' His smile faded a little. Was he confused? Good, she thought. He could join the club.

But maybe she needed to explain. It was only fair.

'I'd started going out with Paul just before Corey came back. Just before Corey died,' she told him. 'He understood…why I held Corey that night. Paul's been wonderful.'

'You're engaged?'

'I won't get engaged until after the baby's born.'

'But you love him?'

She stiffened at that. 'I don't see that that concerns you.'

'No.' His smile returned, teasing, and she thought suddenly that he'd make a great family doctor. He'd have people telling him anything he asked.

She sighed. OK, there was no reason why she shouldn't tell him. It was no great secret.

'I…I'm fond of Paul,' she told him. 'But I'm carrying another man's baby. I want Paul to go into it with his eyes wide open. I want to see how he feels about the baby after the birth. He wants to marry me now but I need him to wait.' She needed to wait, too, she thought, but she wasn't going into that.

There was a pucker now between Dev's eyebrows. It happened when he was trying to figure things out. She liked it, she decided. She'd like to touch it…

Down, girl, she told herself. What was happening here? Hormones? At seven months pregnant? Get real.

'I see,' Dev said softly, and she bit her lip.

'Paul might even come out for the birth,' she said, trying to sound cheerful. Trying to sound like this was just a normal, run-of-the-mill regular conversation. 'He's trying to figure things out now. He's an orthopaedic surgeon at the hospital where I work so he has major work commitments. But he's really upset that I'm stuck here.'

'I'd imagine he must be.'

'But he agrees that I need to get a flat in Brisbane for the duration,' she said, still trying to sound positive. Cheerful. Like things were totally under control.

Trying not to think how bleak a flat in Brisbane sounded.

'Why would you want to get a flat in Brisbane?' Dev demanded.

Emma thought. Good question. But she'd talked it through with Paul. It really was the most sensible thing to do and if he managed to come out...

That should make it seem less bleak.

It didn't.

'I'll wait there for the birth,' she told Dev. 'Paul's checked and he says Brisbane has a first-rate hospital.'

'This is a first-rate hospital,' Dev retorted. 'Harriet has said she'll deliver you, and I can back her up.'

'I can't stay here.'

'My mother will break her heart if you don't.'

She hesitated. She'd wanted to introduce her baby to this family, but just how immersed did she want to become?

And the way she was feeling about Dev...

The inexplicable way she was feeling about Dev...

'Dev, I'm not sure. Is this wise?' she asked, meeting his look head on. 'Lorna's been lovely. I know you guys would have me to stay. But...'

'She needs you to stay.'

'I can't stay for ever.'

'But you can stay until Lorna's grandchild is born,' he told her, and his hand came out and caught hers. It was a gesture of urgency, and it caught her off guard. She felt her fingers slip into

No. More and more she knew that it wasn't. It was different.

It was crazy.

He was asking her to stay. What choice did she have? she thought bleakly. An apartment in Brisbane, or stay here? To stay near Lorna. And…Dev?

'Is there somewhere here I can stay?'

'Our family home is huge. Vast. It's a bit ramshackle but it's a great place to stay. My father was the town doctor and his father before him. My grandpa had eight kids. Honestly, there's heaps of room.'

'I…' She tried to think. 'Maybe.'

'Good.' He smiled then, that special, heart-stopping smile that swept all before it. 'I'll take you home tomorrow morning.'

'Hey.' She stared at him, astounded. 'I said maybe. How did we suddenly get from A to Z without any apparent path in between? What about your mother?'

'My mother will love you to bits. You know that.'

'I…' She stared wildly up at him. 'I can't.'

'Of course you can. Why not?'

There must be a hundred reasons. A thousand reasons.

He was still holding her hand.

his and she felt the warmth of him seep into her. The strength. 'You must.'

'Why must I?' She tugged at her hands but she wasn't released.

He hesitated. And then, with the attitude of a man who'd decided to tell it like it was, he released her hands and turned to the window.

'Em, since Corey's illness, I think my mother's been to the brink of madness and back.'

'I can understand—'

'I'm not sure that you can.' He had his back to her. His shoulders were squared, as if he was remembering pain. Bracing himself against it.

'Corey's illness was diagnosed when he was almost through medical school,' he said softly, as if every word was torn from him. 'He didn't want anyone to know—but, of course, my mother had to know. The police contacted her when he had his first manic episode. She went down to Brisbane, she got him sorted, she stayed with him until he was settled on medication, and she didn't tell anyone. My father…my father had a weak heart and she worried that the strain would kill him. I'd already qualified and I was in the US, doing further training. So my mother took it on herself to act as a barrier between Corey and the rest of us.'

'She didn't tell you at all?'

'She told my father that Corey had had pneumonia, which was why she'd had to go to him.

That was all. It was…stupid. We maybe could have helped. If we'd known…'

'Maybe no one could have helped Corey,' Emma said softly. She gazed at his back, knowing the pain he was feeling. It was the same pain she'd felt when Corey had walked away.

'Anyway, as soon as he qualified he left for overseas.' Dev sighed. 'As I had. Then, no matter where he was in the world, no matter where I travelled, we always seemed to miss each other. I didn't see until later how carefully orchestrated that was. He told Mum that things were OK and she believed him—she wanted to believe him. She didn't realise how appallingly insidious this damned disease is.'

'So you suspected nothing?'

'When Corey rang me to tell me he was going to Ethiopia, he sounded…well, he sounded strung up enough to make me worry. But I thought maybe he'd had a love affair that had gone wrong or something. I told him that I'd come and visit and he told me no. The next time I rang he told me that he'd just met a girl and she was wonderful and my coming might mess things up. He told me to let him be.'

'I guess…I hope that was me.'

'Yeah. I guess. But then my father died and he didn't come home. He was in England by then.'

Was that what had pushed him over the edge? Emma wondered. She'd been ill. Corey had taken her back to England. If he'd got a phone call out of the blue saying his father had died…

She winced.

But Dev had moved on. 'I found him soon aft that,' he told her. 'He'd registered to work England so I found him through the hospital was working in. But when I phoned and tried talk to him, he was just…manic. And finally mother told me.'

'Oh, Dev.' Hell. This damned illness hurt many, she thought bleakly. It could be as bad cancer. Just as deadly. 'I'm so sorry.'

'It's not your place to be sorry,' he told her, he turned to face her. 'But you can help. mother still blames herself for not telling Dad me. The fact that Corey wouldn't let me close when I did know is irrelevant. As I said, she's to the brink of despair. So…' He spread his h 'Emma, stay here for the birth of her grand Let her see that there's something good come all of this. Please?'

She stared up into his face, confused. S fused. Confused and confused and confused

But it wasn't just the events of the past th her confused. It was the way this man loo her.

Was it because he was like Corey?

his and she felt the warmth of him seep into her. The strength. 'You must.'

'Why must I?' She tugged at her hands but she wasn't released.

He hesitated. And then, with the attitude of a man who'd decided to tell it like it was, he released her hands and turned to the window.

'Em, since Corey's illness, I think my mother's been to the brink of madness and back.'

'I can understand—'

'I'm not sure that you can.' He had his back to her. His shoulders were squared, as if he was remembering pain. Bracing himself against it.

'Corey's illness was diagnosed when he was almost through medical school,' he said softly, as if every word was torn from him. 'He didn't want anyone to know—but, of course, my mother had to know. The police contacted her when he had his first manic episode. She went down to Brisbane, she got him sorted, she stayed with him until he was settled on medication, and she didn't tell anyone. My father...my father had a weak heart and she worried that the strain would kill him. I'd already qualified and I was in the US, doing further training. So my mother took it on herself to act as a barrier between Corey and the rest of us.'

'She didn't tell you at all?'

'She told my father that Corey had had pneumonia, which was why she'd had to go to him.

That was all. It was…stupid. We maybe could have helped. If we'd known…'

'Maybe no one could have helped Corey,' Emma said softly. She gazed at his back, knowing the pain he was feeling. It was the same pain she'd felt when Corey had walked away.

'Anyway, as soon as he qualified he left for overseas.' Dev sighed. 'As I had. Then, no matter where he was in the world, no matter where I travelled, we always seemed to miss each other. I didn't see until later how carefully orchestrated that was. He told Mum that things were OK and she believed him—she wanted to believe him. She didn't realise how appallingly insidious this damned disease is.'

'So you suspected nothing?'

'When Corey rang me to tell me he was going to Ethiopia, he sounded…well, he sounded strung up enough to make me worry. But I thought maybe he'd had a love affair that had gone wrong or something. I told him that I'd come and visit and he told me no. The next time I rang he told me that he'd just met a girl and she was wonderful and my coming might mess things up. He told me to let him be.'

'I guess…I hope that was me.'

'Yeah. I guess. But then my father died and he didn't come home. He was in England by then.'

Was that what had pushed him over the edge? Emma wondered. She'd been ill. Corey had taken her back to England. If he'd got a phone call out of the blue saying his father had died...

She winced.

But Dev had moved on. 'I found him soon after that,' he told her. 'He'd registered to work in England so I found him through the hospital he was working in. But when I phoned and tried to talk to him, he was just...manic. And finally my mother told me.'

'Oh, Dev.' Hell. This damned illness hurt so many, she thought bleakly. It could be as bad as cancer. Just as deadly. 'I'm so sorry.'

'It's not your place to be sorry,' he told her, and he turned to face her. 'But you can help. My mother still blames herself for not telling Dad and me. The fact that Corey wouldn't let me close even when I did know is irrelevant. As I said, she's gone to the brink of despair. So...' He spread his hands. 'Emma, stay here for the birth of her grandchild. Let her see that there's something good come from all of this. Please?'

She stared up into his face, confused. So confused. Confused and confused and confused.

But it wasn't just the events of the past that had her confused. It was the way this man looked at her.

Was it because he was like Corey?

No. More and more she knew that it wasn't. It was different.

It was crazy.

He was asking her to stay. What choice did she have? she thought bleakly. An apartment in Brisbane, or stay here? To stay near Lorna. And…Dev?

'Is there somewhere here I can stay?'

'Our family home is huge. Vast. It's a bit ramshackle but it's a great place to stay. My father was the town doctor and his father before him. My grandpa had eight kids. Honestly, there's heaps of room.'

'I…' She tried to think. 'Maybe.'

'Good.' He smiled then, that special, heart-stopping smile that swept all before it. 'I'll take you home tomorrow morning.'

'Hey.' She stared at him, astounded. 'I said maybe. How did we suddenly get from A to Z without any apparent path in between? What about your mother?'

'My mother will love you to bits. You know that.'

'I…' She stared wildly up at him. 'I can't.'

'Of course you can. Why not?'

There must be a hundred reasons. A thousand reasons.

He was still holding her hand.

'Emma, I need to go,' he told her, and suddenly the businesslike tone disappeared. 'I... Kyle's funeral's in half an hour and I've been asked to speak. But, please. My mother and I need to take care of you. Stay here until Corey's baby's born. Please?'

Emotional blackmail. This was nothing but emotional blackmail.

And there was no answer to give him but yes.

Which was why, at eleven the next morning, she found herself being tucked into Dev's big sedan, clucked over by Janelle and waved goodbye to from by all the hospital staff.

'They're treating me like I'm as fragile as Dresden china,' she said a trifle crossly as Dev turned out of the parking lot.

'You saved Suzy's life. You'll find the whole town will treat you as precious.'

'Suzy...' She hesitated.

'Suzy is fine. I checked with the Brisbane surgical team this morning. She'll need a couple of sessions with a plastic surgeon but they're confident she'll end up with only hairline scars. Nothing else. Jodie's great. Colin's fine.' He hesitated as he looked across at her. 'We were so lucky. Without you...'

'Without me the truck wouldn't have swerved and everyone would be fine.'

'The truck was on the wrong side of the road. If he hadn't hit you first, he would have hit the school bus. Head on. It's odds on that you single-handedly saved a score of lives.'

'Except Kyle's.'

'As you say.' His face set and she knew he was thinking of yesterday. The whole hospital had been silent for the time it had taken for Kyle to be buried.

This was a small town. Every death affected everybody. For Emma, who'd never known such care, the feeling was stunning.

'The funeral was bad?' she said tentatively, and he grimaced. But then his grimace turned to a sort of smile.

'Yeah, but they were great,' he told her. 'Kyle's whole family. They just celebrated his life in such a great way.' He turned to her and he managed a crooked smile. 'You know, you gave them a gift. Letting them say goodbye.'

'You would have done the same.'

'I might not have done it with such compassion,' he said softly. 'I might not have thought about it. It's not something that's taught in medical school—lessons in grief.'

'It should be.'

'Maybe it's something that can't be taught. Maybe it's something you need to learn the hard way.'

'Then by rights,' she said softly, 'you should have it in spades.'

'Yeah.' He turned to face the road but his hands gripping the steering-wheel were clenched white.

'What were you doing overseas?' she asked. This conversation was too heavy by far, It was time to lighten up.

'Oncological surgery mostly. Brain tumours in kids.'

'Goodness.' She thought about it for a bit. 'Um…goodness. That's a far cry from country medicine.'

'I guess.'

'So you were practising overseas?'

'I was learning.'

'Where?'

He told her the name of the clinic—the most prestigious medical establishment in the US—and she took a deep breath or two.

'Impressive.' She was definitely impressed.

'Interesting.'

'So you came home…'

'When my father died,' he said bluntly. 'I came home for Dad's funeral and Corey didn't. Mum couldn't keep his illness from me any more. After that I… It was impossible to go back.'

'So you're stuck here,' she said thoughtfully. 'Same as me.'

'I wouldn't say that.'

'You don't miss your work?'

'There are things here to make up for it.' He managed a half-smile. 'There are always things to make up for it.'

'So you're making the best of it.'

'I guess.' But the knuckles on the steering-wheel were still white. There were demons driving this man, Emma thought. How trapped was he?

They drove in silence for a bit. Down the same cliff road where the bus had crashed. They passed the spot, and there were a couple of smashed posts and railing. Nothing else.

Scars healed. Life went on.

Two minutes later they turned onto a rough track leading to the sea.

Was this where he lived? 'This is a long way out of town for the doctor's residence.'

'It's a bit inconvenient,' he said brusquely. 'It's been great. In the past. But I'm thinking of moving.'

It's been great. There was an understatement. They pulled to a halt. Emma gazed out at the house. It was beautiful.

'Wow,' she said inconsequentially, and there was that half-smile again.

'As you say.'

She wasn't listening.

They'd pulled off the main road and bumped along a track two hundred or so yards long—a track that was more a tunnel through the rainforest. Then they'd emerged to sunshine. The house was old and rambling, a sprawling weatherboard homestead that would have been just as at home on a vast country property as it was here. It was on a bluff, backed by the sea, a tiny pocket of flat land tucked between the hills that had scooped down to form a creek bed, running beside the house. The creek rippled over smooth stones to merge into the waves in the cove beyond.

And the garden…

The garden was a wilderness of bougainvillea, towering gums, crimson grevillea and a mass of rambling roses spilling out from the veranda, merging into the mass of undergrowth beyond. The garden looked desperately in need of attention if some of the lovely things there were to survive much longer, but nothing could detract from its wild magnificence.

And beyond the garden—the sea. The cove was a stretch of golden sand where the boulder-strewn creek-bed merged in shallow ripples into the surf beyond sapphire sea. Emma could scarcely believe it.

She stared around her and it was such a strange feeling. For Emma, who'd never felt as if she belonged anywhere, who'd been independent and alone for so long, this felt like…

Home.

'This is paradise,' she breathed.

'It is.' He did smile then, and this was no half-smile. 'Do you think you can bear to stay here until your baby is born?'

'If I have to,' she breathed. 'Oh, Dev.' She climbed from the car and gazed around her with awe. 'It's just lovely.'

'Come inside.' He was still smiling. 'My mother will be here soon. She's promised she'd come to see you installed.'

'Your mother?' She frowned a bit more. 'Um…doesn't Lorna live here?'

The smile died. 'Not any more.'

'What do you mean?' she asked. 'Not any more?'

'After my father and then Corey died,' he said softly, 'she couldn't bear it. Too many ghosts.'

'That's crazy,' she told him. 'Ghosts are wonderful.' She climbed the steps to the veranda and gazed around, smelling the roses and the salt of the sea. There were vivid green lorikeets in the bougainvillea, swinging like trapeze artists along the veranda posts. They were distracting. This feeling that she belonged here was distracting.

She needed to concentrate.

'I thought Lorna lived here.'

'I'm sorry. Didn't she say?'

'Lorna told me I had to come and stay here. I assumed…'

'You assumed wrong.'

She thought about it. 'So it's just you and me.'

'That's right.' He frowned. 'I assumed you wouldn't be nervous, but maybe I should have warned you. It's lovely but it's lonely. I'm not home all that often.'

'Is Margaret happy about this?'

'Margaret?'

'Your fiancée,' she said patiently, and his face closed.

'Margaret's not my fiancée.'

'Not?'

'No.'

She stared. 'Well, you could have fooled me,' she retorted. 'Everyone at the hospital says you two are getting married.'

'We haven't decided to get married.'

She sighed. Glanced again at the lorikeets. Glanced again at the sea.

Maybe she shouldn't stay here. 'Look, things are… Maybe we need to get things straight. I'm confused. If I were Margaret…'

'I'm not about to ravish you.'

'I'm not expecting to jump you either,' she retorted. 'But I don't know how happy Paul's going to be about me sharing a house with you for a couple of months. Alone.'

'I'd imagine Paul trusts you.'

'Oh, for heaven's sake. He trusts me so much that carrying another man's child hasn't affected how he feels about me,' she snapped. 'But I'm not pushing it.'

'There's not a lot of choice,' he told her. 'You did decide to come here when you were seven months pregnant. Hardly a sensible choice.'

This man was being seriously irritating. Seriously disconcerting. He stood there sounding so darned reasonable—as if he would have managed things so much better—and all she wanted to do was to hit him.

Hit him? Maybe not. Maybe something else.

Cut it out, Emma, she told herself. Blasted pregnancy hormones. Blasted…something.

'It was pretty dumb,' he added, and she firmed in her intention. Hormones or not, definitely the impulse was definitely to slug the guy.

'I know it was hardly sensible,' she said through gritted teeth. 'Sensible? Ha. It was daft. But I'm paying. I'm stuck here in this godforsaken place…'

'Godforsaken?'

'Well, ends of the earth.'

'You know, we've been offered a fortune for this house,' Dev said cautiously. 'Lots of people would pay big money to stay here.'

'I'm not lots of people.'

'Well, you are two people.' He was smiling. He thought it was funny, she realised. But then he added, more seriously, 'But, no, you're not lots of people. Most people in the world don't get invited to stay.'

'Like Margaret?'

They were on dangerous ground again. His face closed.

'Emma,' he said cautiously, 'if we're to share a house for two months, maybe we'd better learn that there are some boundaries we shouldn't cross.'

'Is discussion of Margaret a boundary?'

'Yeah, I think she's off limits.'

'But you are going to marry her?'

'I don't have a… It's none of your business.'

'The whole town thinks you're going to marry her.'

'The whole town would,' he said, exasperated. 'Now, do you mind? I need to get back to the hospital.'

'You want to dump me and run.'

'Yes,' he said, even more exasperated. He swung open the screen door leading into the house. 'If you'll stop speculating on my love life for five minutes, I'll give you a guided tour.'

'I'm coming.' She stared around once more in awe before she went inside. In truth, the cheek she'd been giving him had been as much a product of nerves as anything. This place was extraordinary. And to think she was going to live here for two months…

With Dev.

Don't go there. Think of practicalities.

What was she going to do here? she wondered. Sleeping in the sun wasn't her scene. 'I might be bored,' she said cautiously, and he sighed.

'I'll organise you membership of the local library. Come inside.'

She walked past him, brushing against him as she went. Drat, she shouldn't have done that. There it was again, this frisson of electricity she couldn't understand. It happened every time she touched him.

Every time he smiled.

She took a deep breath and walked inside.

And stopped.

'Oh.'

'What's wrong?'

'I… It's very nice.'

It wasn't.

From the outside the house had looked big and rambling and welcoming. Inside, it was anything but welcoming.

Every blind had been pulled. Open doors led to two big sitting rooms—or maybe one was a study—off the front entrance. Who would know what they were used for? There was only sparse furniture, and what there was seemed to be covered in dustsheets.

The blinds were obviously closed all day. They'd been scorched by the sun and had started to perish. The morning sun was glinting in through the tattered slits where they'd given up holding onto themselves. Ugh.

The place looked dreary. Empty.

Desperately in need of paint.

But Dev wasn't giving her time to investigate. 'I don't use these rooms. I have a bedroom here but apart from that I live out the back.' He was ushering her along the wide passage that ran through the length of the house.

'Good,' she managed. 'I can't imagine you living here.'

Out the back was better, but only marginally. The kitchen at least did look used. This was a room that could easily hold a vast dining table and settees on the side. It was huge.

It was empty.

There was an ancient blackened woodstove, unused.

There was a nasty modern cooker in the corner—cheap—and a microwave.

There was no vast dining table. Instead, there was a little laminated four-seater, the type you bought in prebuilt furniture stores.

'Ugh,' she said before she could help herself, and Dev sighed.

'Yeah, it's pretty terrible. After my father and Corey died...well, my mother found everything reminded her of how things had been. She stripped the house of everything that reminded her of them. Then she still couldn't bear it so she moved. Everything she hadn't got rid of already she seemed to need in her new unit and I haven't seen the need to buy more.'

'Why not?'

He sighed. 'Well, maybe the ghosts are here for me, too. Maybe it's time I moved on.'

'But it's gorgeous.'

'It's empty.'

'You could fill it again.'

'I don't need to just for me. It's adequate.'

'Adequate for two days,' she retorted, staring around in distaste. The place looked barren. 'I can't live here for two months.'

'Redecorate if you like,' he said indifferently. 'I'm happy to pay for it.'

She eyed him cautiously. 'If I'm living here for two months, I'll pay to redecorate it myself,' she told him. 'You sound like you won't notice if I do.'

'I use this place to sleep,' he told her, still indifferent. 'There's too much medicine in this town for one doctor to handle. I work. When I manage to get a locum I go to the city. I don't stay here.'

She stared around her some more. She walked across to the window and pushed aside the old gingham curtains. Once they'd had ties that had held them back. They would have been pretty, she thought. Cheerful. But the ties were long gone, which meant the window was permanently curtained.

Permanently closed.

And outside was the sea and the mountains. Outside was blocked out by neglect.

'I bet this place used to be fantastic,' she said softly, and Dev's face closed.

'Yes. When my father and Corey were alive. They were…great.'

'Yeah, they were great but now they're dead,' she said, exasperated. 'So what about this house? Does it have to be dead, too?'

'I—'

'Corey would have hated this.'

'You don't know what Corey would have hated. Now, if we can—'

'Hey, I do know what Corey would have hated,' she snapped. 'Let's not do the ''please don't speak of the dead'' thing to me. He was your brother. He was my husband. He was ill and now he's dead. But if you think he'd like a mausoleum in his honour, you're badly mistaken.'

'I didn't think he'd like a mausoleum. This is not about Corey.'

'No?'

'No.'

'So you're not living like this because you're mourning Corey or your father. What, then? Your career?'

'Will you butt out?'

'I never have,' she told him. 'I don't know why I should start now.'

He started at her, seemingly exasperated. Then he sighed. 'Look, this is stupid.'

'It is, isn't it?' she agreed.

'I didn't mean the house. I meant us disagreeing. We need to learn to live in some sort of agreement.'

'Yeah, we do.'

'So can we get on with it?' he asked. He glanced at his watch. 'I need to go. It's past eleven already. I have house calls and afternoon clinic. My mother will drop a casserole off some time soon. I may or may not be back for dinner. Can you cope?'

She drew a deep breath. 'What, cope with sitting round waiting for a casserole?'

'What else do you want?'

'I don't know,' she told him. 'But you go on back to work. I'll just stay here and figure it out.'

*   *   *

Maybe an apartment in Brisbane would be preferable to this.

Once Dev had gone, Emma wandered through the big house and the emptiness echoed round and round her. The house smelled musty and unloved but it had such potential. The sound of the surf was washing gently through the windows. The lorikeets in the bougainvillea were squawking their delight as they drank the nectar.

The bougainvillea was a problem, she thought. It looked gorgeous but it had become overgrown so it was blocking the windows. Even when she'd hauled back the curtains, the house was dark.

She was expected to sit here for two months and calmly wait for her baby? She'd go nuts.

Emma had grown up with the work ethic drilled into her from the time she could crawl. An idle hand was a sinful hand, her parents had decreed. So was she to be sinful?

Maybe not sinful. Maybe just confused?

An idle hand was a confused hand.

That'd be right. She'd never stopped. She'd worked hard for her medical degree. She'd thrown herself into medicine. She'd worked up until the day she'd got on a plane to come out here.

Now what?

Take a rest?

OK, she needed to slow down for a few more days, she conceded. Harriet had been right to force her to stop. She didn't want to risk this baby.

'But I can't sit here and vegetate. By myself.

'Dev might be home for dinner.

'Gee, that's great. I can have the table set for him and his slippers warmed.'

Ha!

What else?

She needed to do something about her clothes. She stared down at the shapeless maternity smock she was wearing. It was the best the town could offer, but it wasn't what she would call attractive.

Well, it's no use getting anything else, she told herself. Not when she was the shape of an elephant and hoping to subside in a matter of weeks.

So what else to do?

There was a tentative knock on the door. Emma took a deep breath. This would be Lorna. Bearer of the casserole. That had to stop, she told herself. She needed to figure out a way to get herself independent. Maybe she could hire another car.

Or maybe not. She'd notified the hire car company of the crash while she'd been in hospital and their reaction had been less than enthusiastic.

Sigh.

Did people who squashed one hire car get to hire another? she wondered. No matter. If she couldn't hire one then she'd just have to buy one, she told herself. There was no way she was staying dependent.

But for now she still needed to accept help. She walked to the door, fixed a grateful smile on her face and swung it wide.

It wasn't Lorna.

It was Katy. Her helper at the crash site.

The little girl was standing on the veranda looking as if she was unsure whether she should be here or not. She had the look of a child who might bolt for cover at any minute.

The last time Emma had seen Katy she had been dressed in her school uniform. Now she was wearing shorts and T-shirt and sandals. Her hair was still hauled into those too-tight plaits, and her thick glasses were low on her freckled nose, increasing her impression of owlishness. When Emma answered the door she took a couple of steps back, as if preparing to run.

'H-hi,' she said.

'Katy.' Emma greeted her with real pleasure. She'd thought of this child a lot these last few days but hadn't had the energy to do anything about finding her. 'Come in.'

'I just… Mum said I had to come and see if you needed anything,' Katy told her.

'You live close?'

'We're just on the other side of the hill.'

'And you're not in school?'

'School finishes for the holidays tomorrow.' Katy was speaking in a forced whisper, as if she was still unsure of her ground. 'But most of the kids on the bus aren't going back until next term. Mr Jeffries is in hospital in Brisbane. He's got a broken shoulder bone as well as a cut face. So we're staying home. Some of us went to Kyle's funeral yesterday. But I... I... Mum said... But if you don't want anything...'

Katy's face was shuttered behind her glasses. There was real pain here, Emma thought. Trauma.

'Did someone talk through what happened with you?' she asked gently. 'Did a counsellor come to the school?'

'I didn't go back to school.'

'But...'

'Dr O'Halloran rang Mum and Dad and said I ought to see someone,' Katy whispered. 'But Dad said there were kids worse off than me who needed it more.' She stared up at Emma, her owlish eyes expressionless. 'I wasn't hurt.'

Why did she suddenly want to gather this child to her and hug her? Not hurt? There were levels and levels of hurt. What Emma was seeing was a layer of damage far deeper than surface pain.

'Did your mum and dad talk to you about what happened?'

'Dad says least said soonest mended.'

'Sometimes that works,' Emma said diffidently. And sometimes it was the stuff of nightmares.

Mostly it was the stuff of nightmares.

'You want a drink?' she asked.

Katy stared up at her and thought about it. 'What do you have?' she asked at last, and the whisper was almost breaking into a normal tone. This was safe ground.

'I have no idea. I'm about to find out. I've just arrived so this is an adventure.'

'Why is it an adventure?'

'Well, this place is like a deserted palace.'

'It's not deserted. Dr O'Halloran lives here.'

'No. Dr O'Halloran sleeps here. There's a difference.' She frowned. 'Katy, what are you doing over the holidays?'

'Nothing. I mean…'

'Do you want a job?'

'A job?' The child stared up at her, confused.

But Emma was moving on. This could suit them all. For Katy to spend her holidays with nothing to do but think of the trauma of the last few days was asking for real long-term trouble. And she needed help herself.

Truth to tell, she could do with a little counselling herself. And if not counselling—at least some company.

'I've got a job that needs doing,' she told the child. 'You might have noticed that I'm having a baby. I'm not allowed to do any physical work. But there's so much to do here. I need hands. I need you and any other kid that was on that bus who feels like helping me out.'

Katy stared. 'Doing what?'

'Cleaning. Polishing. Sweeping. Gardening. Painting. Dr O'Halloran says I can do what I want with this place. Does it look dreary to you?' She flung open the front door to its full extent and waved to the inside. 'What do you think?'

Katy peered into the first two doors. She looked doubtfully up at Emma as if she couldn't believe that an adult could really be asking her opinion.

Emma wrinkled her nose and gestured for her to look further.

So Katy walked down the passage and opened the next two doors. Here was an unused bedroom, stripped completely of furniture, and the room that Dev had told Emma she could use. Emma's room contained furniture, but only just. One single bed. One dresser. The room was painted a pretty blue but its walls had obviously once been covered with pictures. The paintings had gone—who knew where?—and all that was left were blank rectangles where they'd hung.

'It's horrid,' Katy said slowly, and Emma beamed.

'There. That's two of us with the same opinion. That's consensus. Do you want the job?'

'Like a real job?' Katie asked cautiously. 'I don't think I'm allowed to get a real job.'

'If you're interested, I'll need to talk to your parents,' Emma told her, thinking fast as she talked. 'There's a bit of planning to do. But I'm thinking... One of the nurses at the hospital told me about a new adventure park on the south coast about fifty miles from here. Do you know it?'

'Adventure World,' Kate breathed. 'It's just opened. Everyone wants to go there. But...' Her face clouded. 'Dad says it's too expensive.'

'Well, how about we talk to the other kids and see what we can do,' Emma said decisively. It could work. It would get these kids together and give them a plan for the holidays—a way to stop them internalising their grief and their trauma—and it could just be a whole lot of fun. 'I need to talk to Dr O'Halloran and his mother,' she went on. 'But the garden's desperate. I don't see how they can object.'

'To what?'

'To a working bee. No. To a whole working hive. And if it works out...if you and anyone else wants to help, then at the end of the holidays we'll run a trip to Adventure World as payment.'

'But why?' Katy was back to whispering again but it wasn't fear that was making her whisper now. It was awe.

Emma stared around her. Why?

Should she be truthful?

Yes.

'Because this place seems like a home—only it isn't. It's stopped after someone died and it shouldn't have. As life shouldn't stop now because Kyle's died. We'll work and we'll have fun and we'll do it in Kyle's honour. We'll ask all Kyle's brothers and sisters to come with us to Adventure World. They can help here, too, if they like. We'll call this the Kyle project—to transform Dr O'Halloran's garden and maybe his house, too. Do you think Kyle would approve?'

Katy's eyes were huge. She considered. She took her time to consider. But finally she made up her mind.

'Kyle would think it was fun,' she decided.

'Well, there you go, then,' Emma said. 'Excellent.' Boy, she was getting involved here, she thought. Involved up to her neck. But it seemed right. She needed company—desperately. These kids needed to do something together, and they needed to bring their thoughts of Kyle out into the open.

Dev mightn't like it. This was Dev's house.

Nope, she thought suddenly. It was Dev and Corey's home—or it should be. She knew that Corey must have loved this place and she was carrying Corey's child. It felt like home. It felt so much like home. She thought of Corey as he'd been so fleetingly and she knew exactly what he'd say. Go for it.

OK, Corey, I will. She grinned—and then there was another knock. 'This will be Dev's mother,' she told Katy. 'Mrs O'Halloran. Let's tell her what we intend doing. If Lorna has no objections, let's get started.'

CHAPTER SIX

THE phone call from his mother consisted of six stunned words.

'She wants to redecorate the house.'

'I told her she could.' Dev was in the middle of applying a cast, balancing his cellphone on his shoulder as he soaked fibreglass-impregnated strips.

There was a long silence on the end of the line. Time to wrap another layer.

'Mum?'

'I… I'm here. She wants to redecorate the house.'

Dev sighed. Where was the cheerful, vital woman he'd lived with and loved for all those years? His father's death and then Corey's had knocked the stuffing out of her. Now something like this had the power to leave her disoriented and confused.

'Mum, it's OK. But I can't talk now. We'll figure things out tonight.'

'But she wants to start now. And you have no idea…'

'Do you not want her to redecorate?'

'No. I mean… It doesn't matter. I don't like that house.'

'I'm sure you do,' Dev said, his voice gentling. 'And if you don't want Emma touching it, we'll tell her not to. I'm sure she'll understand.'

'It's good that she's touching it. I mean, what she's doing—it's good, but…'

'She's not physically working, is she?' Hell, the last thing he wanted was for Emma to be hauling furniture. She could get decorators in. But where would you find a decorator in Karington?

Apparently she wasn't talking decorators. 'No, but you should see what she's organised. Dev, I don't know…I mean…'

'You don't want her in the house?'

'I didn't say that.' His mother sounded as if she was torn between laughter and tears.

He was being eyed with impatience. Joey Baird had broken his arm in the crash. The swelling had now subsided and Dev was replacing his holding slab with a more permanent cast. The cast was drying while he talked.

'Mum, can we talk about this tonight?' he asked again. 'I'll drop in after work.'

'You'd better go straight home after work,' his mother retorted. 'Oh, Dev…'

'Oh, Dev, what?'

'Just, oh, Dev.'

*   *   *

So three hours later he drove towards home in some trepidation. It was just before dusk—almost eight. He'd finished for the night. He'd dropped in on his mother and found her uncommunicative and sleepy.

Maybe Emma would be the same. Maybe Emma would already be in bed. That way...

That way what?

He wouldn't have to see her?

Why didn't he want to see her?

The problem was that he *did* want to see her, he decided, and suddenly his thoughts seemed almost savage. His hands gripped the steering-wheel and he stared out through the gathering dusk and the vision of Emma was right there before him.

Emma was carrying Corey's child.

The knowledge was creating a jumble of conflicting emotions he didn't know how to deal with.

Corey. Emma. Corey's child.

Corey had loved Emma.

Well, why wouldn't he? he asked the dusk. Anyone would love Emma. She has such life. Such spirit. Such courage.

She has a steady, safe and 'wonderful' boyfriend called Paul somewhere back in the UK, just waiting for her to deliver her baby so he can marry her.

So...what?

So why didn't he want to go home to her?

Why the hell were his hands gripped the steering-wheel so hard that they hurt?

This was crazy. He was a grown man. He had a life. Emma was a relative—of sorts—staying with him for the next couple of months. Nothing more.

His cellphone crackled into use through the car speakers.

'Dev?'

'Margaret.' It was almost a relief to hear her.

'Have you finished for the night?'

'Mmm.'

'You're going home?'

'I think I should,' he told her. 'Emma's there.'

There was a tiny silence and he thought suddenly of what Emma had asked him—whether Margaret would be happy about them sharing a house.

He still thought it was a dumb question, didn't he? Why wouldn't Margaret be happy? How could it possibly bother her?

Maybe it did.

'How about driving round and having supper with us?' he told her. That'd get things off on the footing he wanted. He might not have decided definitely that Margaret was fiancée material, but Emma had a boyfriend and…well, he had Margaret.

'Do you want me to?' Margaret asked.

'Of course I do,' he told her—more warmly than he meant to. Uh-oh. Why had he done that? He didn't want to raise any expectations.

The expectations had already been raised and he knew it.

'Well, I will,' Margaret told him. 'When do you want me?'

'Give me half an hour.'

'I'll bring supper,' she told him. 'And a bottle of wine.'

'Great.'

It *was* great, he decided as he ended the call. He'd organised support. Now all he had to do was go home and face Emma.

Dev turned the car round the last bend and stopped short. Emma wasn't in bed.

No one was in bed.

Every light in the place was on, and there were people everywhere.

He pulled to a halt and stared in amazement. There had to be six or eight cars parked in front of the house. And the veranda... The veranda seemed to have become a storeroom, with furniture piled high and spilling down onto the steps.

There were people walking out the front door, kids with attached parents. He pulled to a halt and stared as they emerged, recognising families he knew.

These were the kids that had been on the bus. Kids with their parents.

Joss Reynolds, father of Jemima, grabbed his hand and gripped it hard as he reached the veranda.

'Doc. Good to see you. I can't tell you how grateful we are that this is happening. Jemmy was just sitting on her bed staring at the wall when Katy rang. We've been that worried. Anyway, the minute Jem heard it was like a light globe went on again. Jem wanted to start now. All the kids did. They've been working like Trojans.'

'They've been working?'

'Since lunchtime.' Joss beamed. 'We said they could stay until six but then the mums got together and organised supper and…well, now we're taking the kids home fed, tired and happy. They'll sleep tonight and for most of them I reckon it's the first time they'll sleep since the bus smash.' He reached down and scooped eight-year-old Jemima up into his arms. 'Come on, missy. If you want to be back here at ten tomorrow, you need to come home now.'

And that was pretty much the story he had from every one of them. Dev stood at the bottom of the stairs as family after family filed past, gripping his hand, expressing their gratitude for something he didn't understand.

Even Kyle's dad tried to thank him.

'We can't tell you what this means,' the man told Dev. He rubbed a hand across eyes that were still swollen from days of weeping. 'Katy rang Sarah, and Sarah and Pete decided they wanted to come straight away.' He gestured to his two oldests who were walking in front of him to the car. 'And I reckon the littlies will be here tomorrow as well. I... The missus... It means so much. What you guys are doing for all of us...' He choked and gripped Dev's hand and then went to join his kids.

Dev stared after him in disbelief. He watched in silence until the last of the cars had disappeared down the track and then he turned—to find Emma standing above him on the veranda.

She looked...guilty?

'What on earth have you been doing?' he managed.

She ventured an uncertain smile. 'Um, organising?'

'I can see that. Would you care to tell me exactly what it is you're organising?'

'Your house. And your garden. But it seems to have got a bit out of hand.' Her smile wavered a bit and she looked so much like a naughty child that he almost smiled back. Almost.

'We've started on the Corey and Kyle memorial project,' she told him, and all impulse to smile died right there.

'The Corey and Kyle memorial project?'

'What we're doing here.'

'With my house.'

'I sort of thought I might explain before I started,' she told him. 'I know I should have. But once Lorna agreed, Katy got really enthusiastic and she started ringing kids and suddenly there were all these parents dropping kids off. And they were so keen. Well, we just had to start. I didn't have the heart to say we had to wait.'

'Doing what?' he asked, with misgivings.

'You did say…' she said cautiously.

'Just tell me.' He was still at the bottom of the steps, staring up at her like he could hardly believe she was there. She looked…astonishing. Madge's maternity dress. Bare feet. Curls tied up with bright red ribbon.

Astonishing.

'Well, some of the older kids are slashing bougainvillea from the windows,' she told him, seemingly unaware of his stupefaction. 'The dads are helping. Me and the littler kids have been hauling out all of the furnishings in preparation for painting. I know you've got rid of heaps of stuff but there still seems plenty left to shift.' She flashed him a doubtful glance and then went on in a hurry. 'We haven't touched your bedroom, of course,' she assured him. 'We thought your bedroom should be out of bounds.'

'Thank you very much.'

He spoke dryly, but there wasn't a hint of remorse in her response. 'Think nothing of it,' she told him with a mischievous chuckle, and he stared up at her as if he was seeing things.

'You think this is funny?'

'Yes.' She met his look square on and her green eyes twinkled. 'Actually, I do. Don't you?'

'I don't know,' he said, goaded. 'You've hauled my furniture onto the veranda and cut back my bougainvillea. You intend to paint. What else?'

'We have a plan.'

'Which is?'

'To redecorate the whole place and make it look cheerful. Inside and out. Your mum's taken every painting off the walls and there are awful blank rectangles all over the house. It looks spooky—like there are ghosts that are just waiting to return. And there are gorgeous things in the garden that are being choked to death. It's so overgrown. Most of the kids want to paint…'

'Most of the kids?'

'This project is open to any kids that were on the bus,' she told him, her laughter fading. 'Dev, these kids have two weeks' holidays and most of them are severely traumatised. What they don't need is two weeks of isolation and boredom while they come to terms in their own way with what's happened. They need to talk it out.'

He took a deep breath. 'Of all the… What the hell gives you the right—?'

'Dev, I'm a paediatrician,' she told him, her voice becoming patient. A reasonable doctor talking to someone with slightly less than average IQ. 'I understand trauma in kids. I'm not a paediatric psychiatrist, but I do know what harm trauma can cause. Paediatrics is what I do. Traumatised kids are my daily work.'

He stared up at her in stunned amazement. She was small and round, swollen with pregnancy. Her jet-black curls, normally a riot around her face, were trying their best to escape their ribbon. Her maternity smock was red and white check. She had a smudge of dirt down one cheek.

She looked like some sort of crazy Christmas parcel, slightly tattered. Left over from last Christmas?

His sense of unreality increased exponentially.

'You're a paediatrician,' he said faintly, and her smile emerged again.

'You knew I was a doctor. What type of doctor did you think I was? Urologist? Geriatrician?'

'I didn't think—'

'No,' she said kindly. 'But that's all right. I'm thinking for you. We can help these kids if all it takes is a splash of paint.'

'You're going to let them paint the whole house?'

'We can always get it painted again,' she said, and suddenly there was a trace of anxiety in her voice. 'If you don't like it, you can repaint. You just…can't tell them you've repainted. They're so enthusiastic. I don't want them to be disappointed.'

He stared at her in exasperation and said the first thing that came into his head. 'Repainting will cost a bomb.'

It was the wrong thing to say. She glowered. 'Right. Is this what you're really worried about? You won't be out of pocket. I'll pay.'

That set him back again. 'How on earth—?'

'I may look tatty.' She glanced down at her appalling smock and gave a rueful grimace. 'Well, OK, I do look tatty, but I'm not an impoverished relative.' She spread her hands in a gesture of pleading. 'I know I'm out of line, Dev, but these kids need this so much. You don't care about the house. I'm stuck here for months. Let me do this. Please?'

She hesitated but when he didn't answer—he couldn't, he hadn't figured out what to say yet— she appeared to force herself to go on. 'Dev, my parents left me wealthy,' she told him diffidently, as if she didn't like admitting it. 'I can afford to transform this place and I'd like to do this very much. Let me. Please.'

'But after two months…'

'When my baby's born, then I'll leave,' she told him. 'Of course I will. You won't be stuck with me for ever. And whatever I do to your house that you hate, of course I'll pay to make it good. But, meanwhile, we can have so much fun.'

Fun.

The word echoed round and round in the still night air.

Fun.

The concept was almost unknown. Dev stared up at her and wondered when fun had last been associated with the way he'd felt about this house?

When had fun last ever been associated with the way he'd ever felt about his life?

Corey's death and his father's death had sucked the joy right out of him, he thought savagely. He felt so responsible. If he could turn back time…

'Come in and have some supper,' she was saying, and he tried to haul his thoughts back together and move forward.

'Margaret's coming,' he told her—almost defiantly—and she smiled.

'That's great. The more the merrier. There's heaps to eat.'

'She's bringing supper with her.'

'We don't need more supper.' She smiled even more and disappeared into the house. He was left to follow. 'Come and see what we have already.'

* * *

They certainly didn't need supper. Every parent seemed to have brought food.

The kitchen had been transformed. Dev's tiny four-seater table and chairs had disappeared. Now there were two vast trestle tables, paint-spattered and workworn, set up to run almost the full length of the kitchen. But they weren't being used for work. The trestles were covered with plates and plates of food. Lamingtons. Sponge cakes. Fairy cakes. Chocolate cake. Bowls and bowls of crisps and nuts and lollies.

'Mary's dad brought the trestles,' Emma told him. 'Aren't they great? We've got ladders, too, and so many paintbrushes I've lost count. And food…'

'Food.' He was starting to sound dumb. He was starting to feel dumb.

'The perishables are in the fridge.' Emma was smiling still more at his look of stupefaction. 'Sausage rolls, little red sausages, you name it.'

'I don't understand.' That was some understatement. 'How…? Why have you done this?'

'It's easy.' She stood on the other side of the trestles and watched his face. Warily, he thought. As if she wasn't quite sure that he wasn't about to jump down her throat. 'Every one of these kids was so shocked that they've been almost immobile. Katy phoned them up and said let's have fun and let's remember Kyle at the same time. So we have. And the parents… Dev, in their way they're as traumatised as their kids. They need to do this almost as much as their children. A community project. Revitalising the doctor's house.'

'But you're in charge,' he said faintly. 'You're doing the organising. You really intend to keep this up?'

'For all of the holidays. Yes.' Her chin jutted in a look of defiance he was starting to recognise. 'At the end of the school holidays we'll go to Adventure World and have a huge Kyle wake.' Her voice was serious again. Steady and determined. 'Dev, I really think it can help.' She hesitated. 'And…if you could join in…it could help you, too.'

That set him back. What the hell was she talking about? 'I don't need help.'

'I think you do,' she said gently. 'I'm sure you do. You and your mother. You can't think of Corey without pain. Without guilt. Do you think he'd want that? To the kids, this is our Kyle project. But to me…I'm doing this partly for me, partly for the kids, but partly for Corey as well. He'd hate that his home was like this. He'd hate that his family was so unhappy.'

'I'm not unhappy.'

'No?'

'Look…' He spread his hands. 'Emma, you mean well, I know, but this is none of your business.'

'Corey was my husband,' she said evenly. 'How he's remembered is very much my business.'

'You're talking about me.'

'Yeah, you seem to be my business, too,' she told him, meeting his look squarely on. 'Somehow.'

'I don't want to be your business.'

'No?' She smiled again, but her face was suddenly less certain. 'Maybe not, but somehow we seem to be stuck with each other.' She picked up a plate and handed it across the trestle. Bread and butter with a scattering of multicoloured sugar droplets. 'This is the best fairy bread,' she said in satisfaction. 'It's really excellent. Try some.'

'My mother said she brought a casserole.' He sounded stiff, he thought. Stupid.

But Emma didn't seem to notice.

'Of course she did,' she told him. 'It's lovely and of course if you want it then you can have it. But if not, it'll freeze. Your mother ate fairy bread like the rest of us.'

'My mother ate fairy bread?' He couldn't believe this.

'She did. She even seemed to enjoy it. As you might. You know, you never know what you're capable of until you try.'

'I don't think I want to try.'

'OK.' She grinned, seemingly not in the least perturbed by his brusqueness, and ate a bit of fairy bread herself while he watched her. He watched her much as he would have if she'd been a coiled snake.

'Do you intend to stay here for ever?' she asked him, between mouthfuls of fairy bread.

'I… No. Yes.' He shook his head. Why the hell were they talking about this? What right did she have to pry?

But she was standing on the other side of the table, her head cocked to one side like an inquisitive sparrow, and she was impossible to ignore. Short of turning around and heading out the door.

And the fairy bread did look good.

But not to start with.

Casserole?

No.

'Did you say there were sausage rolls?' he asked, and her smile widened.

'How did I guess you'd want some? I even kept some warm for you. How good am I?' She bent over, sweeping the floor with the hem of her amazing maternity tent as she retrieved a tray of sausage rolls from the oven. 'Mrs Kipling brought them and they're yummy.'

'Yummy,' he said faintly. He dunked one in ketchup, ate it, thought about it, dunked another and ate it, too. They were actually...yummy.

'You were saying?' Emma said encouragingly.

'I wasn't saying.'

'Yes, you were. When I asked whether you were staying here for ever.'

'Emma...'

'Why won't you tell me?'

Why wouldn't he tell her? Was there a reason?

There wasn't a reason. It was just...she made him feel exposed, he thought. Telling Emma things somehow seemed different to telling anyone else. It was like admitting things to himself.

He couldn't lie to Emma, he thought a little bit desperately. He didn't understand why he felt like this, but talking to Emma seemed as if he was talking to a part of himself that he'd long ago blocked off. That he wasn't at all sure he wanted to expose.

'I'm not sure,' he told her.

'Do you want to stay here?'

'The work I was doing in the States was great.'

'But here... Is the work you're doing here great?'

'My mother needs me to stay. The community needs me. To get another doctor to come to Karington seems impossible.'

'So you're here under duress. Which explains the house.'

'I'm not here under duress.'

'But you haven't accepted that you might enjoy to stay here for ever.'

'For ever's a long time.'

'Or not long enough,' she said softly. 'In the case of Kyle of or Corey, for ever's very short indeed.'

'As you say.' He clipped his words, harsh and hard, trying to shut her up, but she was incorrigible.

'So if you're only going to stay here for, say, two or three months,' she said thoughtfully. 'Like me, for instance. If you're only here for a short time, maybe you could enjoy it?'

Two or three months? Two or three decades more like. 'I can't.'

'You can't enjoy life? That's crazy.'

'Look, just because things have gone your way all your life…'

'Hey.' Her face stilled. 'Things have gone my way?'

'If you can look at life and think that it's all frivolous…'

'I don't.'

He stared at her, trying to see her as she really was. A crazy pixie in a crimson tent. 'You seem…'

'Frivolous?'

'Yes,' he admitted, goaded.

She stared at him, considering. She lifted another piece of fairy bread—and then carefully put it down, as if what she was about to say was too important to do between mouthfuls.

'Dev, my father died of Alzheimer's when I was ten,' she said. She seemed to be choosing each word with care. As if she wasn't used to saying this, and she didn't like saying it now she was. 'You know what Alzheimer's is like. You can guess what my childhood was like. Anyway, after my father died my mother fell to pieces. So I took on the care of my ailing mother until I was twenty-six. I was all she had and she leaned on me absolutely. I didn't have a night free until she died. Not a night out in my life. Then I felt bereft. Lost. So I went to work in Ethiopia and I met and married a man with manic depression. He committed suicide and left me pregnant.' She looked up and met his eyes. 'Yep, my life's been pure frivolity,' she said harshly. 'I can see that.'

He felt like he was backed against a wall with nowhere to go. What he was saying was stupid, but still there was a need to... To what? Push her away? Make her someone who was flippant? Insubstantial?

Not desirable?

'You say you're wealthy.' It was a dumb thing to say. It was all he could think of.

'So that makes me frivolous?'

'You eat fairy bread.' Oh, gee, he was sounding really sensible now. And she saw the absurdity of what he was saying.

She stared at him for a long, long minute. And then those gorgeous green eyes creased into a chuckle. It was a lovely chuckle, warm and resonant, and it resounded around the old kitchen as laughter hadn't resounded in years.

'Guilty,' she told him. 'Guilty, guilty, guilty. Yep, I eat fairy bread any chance I get, so therefore I am frivolous, as accused. Take me away and lock me up.'

'Seriously…'

'No,' she said, but her laughter died. 'No, I won't be serious. Dev, I've had enough of serious in my life to last me a lifetime. I intend to be frivolous whenever I feel like it. Starting now. You want to join me?'

'I…'

'Scared?'

'No,' he said at last. 'I'm not. But I'm being pushed, Emma.'

'I know.' Her voice was suddenly serious. 'I have no right to barge into your life and turn it topsy-turvy. And in normal circumstances I wouldn't. But I'm feeling really bad that I've been thrust on you. I'm feeling bad that I didn't come earlier. I've stuffed things up and I'm trying to make the best of things—as I always have. As you need to learn to do, too. You can't ruin the rest of your life because of guilt about Corey.'

'Why the hell…?'

'You're feeling bad because Corey wouldn't let you close.'

'I beg—'

'Don't go formal on me.' They were still standing—absurdly—on either side of the loaded trestle table. 'We haven't got time. But your mother says you were building a magnificent career while Corey quietly self-destructed, and now you're blaming yourself.'

'I—'

He wasn't allowed to get a word in. 'I was building myself a life, too,' she told him, cutting across his attempt to speak. 'And I knew Corey was ill. But Corey chose not to let me close. You know what? I've decided that Corey only married me because at that time I was needier than he was. He hauled me back to the UK, he got me the best medical attention and then he left me. Any contact I tried to maintain was rejected absolutely. Do you honestly think if you'd known about his illness any earlier he would have let you help?'

'I could have tried.'

'As your mother tried. As I tried. And, believe me, I did try, Dev. I fought every way I knew how to keep him close. But he knew what he was doing. He had enough stable, lucid periods over the years for his choice to be total and worthy of respect. It may not be a decision either of us agreed with, but he had the right to his isolation.'

'I could have helped him.'

'Not unless he wanted you to help, and he didn't. Period. Beating yourself up about it now isn't going to do any good to anyone.'

'So you've just moved on?'

'What choice do I have?' she demanded, exasperated. 'I only get one life. Corey's illness destroyed his joy. Shall I let it destroy me as well? Or this baby I'm carrying? I had a childhood shadowed by illness and by death. I'm damned if I'll let my baby have that shadow as well.'

He stared at her. Her chin was still tilted. Her defiance was absolute.

'So you'll eat fairy bread,' he said faintly.

'Yep. And if you'll let me, I'll paint your living room jonquil yellow.'

'As if I have a choice.'

'Oh, you have a choice,' she told him. 'Look around. There's nothing here that can't be undone at a word from you. We've cleared the rooms. We've brought in trestles and equipment for painting. We've scrubbed and we've got everything ready. We've even ordered a few gallons of paint. But the guy who runs the hardware place—Jack Sims, father of Robbie and Sam—is holding delivery until ten tomorrow. I said we'd run it past you before we made a final decision. So it's up to you, Dev.'

'And if I don't agree?'

'Then I ring the kids and tell them it's not on. And I tell your mother it's not happening. I'm not sure who will be more disappointed.'

'That's blackmail.'

'Yeah, it is,' she said cheerfully. 'Paediatrician holds jonquil-yellow paintbrush to surgeon's head and threatens future by fun. As I said, guilty, guilty, guilty. Can I go ahead, please, sir?'

He glowered and dug his hands deep in his pockets. 'I don't have a choice.'

'Now you're being grumpy.'

'I am not being grumpy.'

'Yes, you are. And ungracious. You want to help me put some plastic wrap over this fairy bread? I don't want it going stale before tomorrow. My workers will need it.'

'Your workers.'

'Twenty kids and associated parents,' she told him, smiling again. 'I've unleashed a monster. All you have to say is go ahead.'

'I don't have a choice.'

'You do have a choice. Grump, grump, grump or join right in and have some fun.'

'You...'

'What?' She smiled at him, a bright, mischievous smile that was teasing all on its own.

He wanted to throw something at her.

Or did he?

She was such an...enigma.

He knew nothing about her, he thought. Or maybe he did. She grinned across at him and the thought was that she was a bright, cheeky flibbertigibbet.

She was wealthy.

She was a paediatrician who'd made a decision to work in developing countries.

She'd supported dying parents.

She was his brother's widow.

And it was the last that shook him most. That was a thought that stayed in his head like a harsh and brutal reality.

This woman was his brother's widow. She was carrying Corey's child. He couldn't...

He didn't want to.

Where the hell were his thoughts headed?

He knew exactly where his thoughts were headed.

There was the sound of a car approaching from outside. Emma glanced through the window, saw the approaching headlights and her shoulders seemed to slump. Just a little.

Fatigue settled over her face, washing away the defiance and the cheerful teasing. How much of this was a cover? he thought. How much did she keep hidden—how she was really feeling?

'You should be in bed,' he said, more roughly than he'd intended.

There was a moment's silence.

'I... Yes,' she said uncertainly, and the fatigue was even more pronounced. 'And here's Margaret. I...I shouldn't be here.'

'Emma...'

'We'll talk about it in the morning.' She faltered. 'If you really don't want me to do this, tell me.'

'Of course I want you to do this.'

She stilled. 'Really?' Her eyes met his, her gaze locking, searching. 'Really, Dev?'

'Really,' he told her, and he was rewarded by her smile. It was a lovely smile, he thought. It was tinged with fatigue. Tinged with tragedy. No, this was no flibbertigibbet. This was...Emma.

'I'll pack up here,' he said, and again his voice was rougher than he'd wanted it to be. 'Go to bed.'

'Thank you,' she whispered. Then, before he knew what she intended, she walked swiftly around the trestle table and stood on tiptoe.

She kissed him lightly, fleetingly—a kiss of friendship. Sister-in-law to brother-in-law.

'Goodnight,' she whispered. 'Thank you, Dev. Sleep well.'

And before he could respond she'd turned and walked out the door.

Leaving him staring after her. With his fingers touching the place on his cheek her lips had touched.

A second kiss.

A kiss to remember?

'It could be wonderful.'

They were sitting on the back step—Margaret and Dev—with Margaret's wine bottle between them, and Margaret was assessing the prospect of having the house redecorated. 'Mind, I don't like jonquil yellow. But you must see, Dev, that this place needs total refurbishment. As long as the children don't do any harm, they can do the bulk of the work and then we can get decorators in afterwards.'

'Yeah.' Dev lifted his wineglass but he didn't drink. He was staring out over the sea. The moon was hanging low over the breakers and the waves were rolling lines of foam surging up the shell-littered beach.

'It's such a lovely place,' Margaret murmured, following his thoughts. 'It's a wonderful place to raise a family.'

A family…

His thought drifted sideways, and stayed. A family.

Maybe he'd been drifting for too long. Letting too many assumptions hang.

'Margaret, do you love me?' Well, there was a crazy question—out of left field. Why the hell had he asked it? And tonight of all nights.

If the assumptions weren't there already, they were now.

Margaret was looking at him in astonishment.

'Of course I do,' she told him. 'Why on earth…?'

'We've never really talked about it,' he said, almost apologetically.

'No, but I always assumed…'

'That I loved you?'

'Don't you?'

He turned to face her. Really faced her. 'I don't know,' he confessed. Well, he may as well be honest. 'I'd always thought it'd be like a bolt of lightning. My parents…they were like two lovers right until the end.'

'I remember,' Margaret said, and there was a tiny trace of something that could almost be reproof in her tone. 'At your father's funeral, your mother was inconsolable.'

'Would you be inconsolable at my funeral?'

'Of course I would.' She was staring at him as if he'd lost his senses. 'Though I might not sob.'

'Sob?'

'Well, your mother was…loud. I mean, she was trying not to be, but…'

'Yeah, she was loud,' Dev said reflectively. 'I remember. Right at the end when we turned to leave the cemetery—yep, she was definitely loud. So you'd do it quietly.'

'This is ridiculous.'

'Indulge me,' he said.

She gave him an odd look. 'OK. I wouldn't do it.' Margaret's voice was suddenly decisive. 'No sobbing. Instead, I'd concentrate on keeping you alive longer. Speaking of which, don't you dare eat any more of that cream cake. Do you know Margery Hollis uses pure cream? Forty-five per cent fat!'

'Arsenic,' Dev said morosely.

'It is.' Margaret hauled the plate away from the bottom step where he'd placed it within arm's reach. 'No more cake. Now, about this love business…'

'This love business…?'

'I don't know about romantic love,' she said. 'But what we have, Dev… It's special.'

'Friendship, you mean?'

'What else would I mean?'

'I don't push your buttons?'

'You're being facetious.'

'I'm just asking.'

'There's no one I'd rather marry than you,' she told him. 'If that's what you mean. As I believe— I hope—there's no one you'd rather marry than me.'

'You think that's a basis for a marriage?'

'Of course it is.' She smiled. 'Dev, where's this going? Are you proposing?'

'I'm not sure,' he told her, trying hard to be honest. 'I don't know. Margaret, I think the sobbing thing might be important.'

'I'll sob if you want me to,' she told him, and she smiled.

'Yeah.' He rose to his feet and stared down at her in the moonlight. She really was beautiful. Slim and beautifully groomed, flawless skin, a wide, lovely smile...

What was there not to like?

Nothing.

All he had to do was say the word.

But he didn't. Instead, he sighed. 'Margaret, it's been a hell of a day.'

'Of course it has,' she told him contritely. She lifted the cream cake—but kept it carefully out of

his range. 'I'll go home and leave you to it. I hope
she's left your bedroom alone.'

'She's left my bedroom alone.'

'You don't want to stay at my place for the duration?'

'I think... She's alone. She's Corey's widow
and she's pregnant. I'd best stay here.'

'You do what you think best,' she told him, and
lifted her face for a goodnight kiss. 'I'll see you
at work tomorrow. And if you like, I'll work on
the sobbing.'

He was out on the veranda alone.

Emma heard Margaret's car take off down the
drive. She listened for his steps. She heard him
climb back up to the veranda.

Nothing.

Nothing, nothing, nothing.

He was out on the veranda alone.

She wanted to be out there with him. She
wanted it so badly it was as if she was being physically pulled.

'You're being ridiculous,' she told the dark,
keeping her toes rigidly under the covers. 'You fell
for Corey and he's like him. But he's nothing like
him.

'No. He's Dev.

'You're marrying Paul.

'You don't know whether you're marrying Paul.

'But you sure as heck know Dev's marrying Margaret.' She was talking to herself, scolding back and forth in the manner she'd learned as a lonely child.

'No, you don't. He mightn't be marrying Margaret.

'So he's going to fall out of love with Margaret and fall into love with the seven-month-pregnant widow of his beloved younger brother.'

She heard what she'd said that time and she heard herself gasp.

'What are you saying? Is that what you want?

'N-no.

'Emma, you're being ridiculous.

'I know I am.

'So go to sleep.

'I can't.

'Ring Paul.

'I don't want to.

'So what are you going to do?

'I'll just lie here awake. And listen to Dev on the veranda. Just for a little…'

CHAPTER SEVEN

LIFE was crazy. Life was a muddle of kids and paint and parents and too much food and a house full of chaos. Life was Emma skipping from project to project. Cajoling kids, helping, getting in the way, giggling, putting Dev's Beatles collection on his stereo and blasting music across the cove. Life was kids covered in paint or kids under vast mounds of gathered weed. Kids racing down to the cove for a swim between tasks, parents rostered to supervise as lifesavers, people wherever he looked.

Life was his mother wandering through the chaos with a look of such bemusement he knew that for the first time since Corey's death she'd been lifted from the tragedy and into life.

Life was his mother's eyes resting with silent pleasure on Emma's swollen figure. Her first grandchild. Child of Corey.

Life was…Emma?

Emma was wherever he looked. Emma was wherever he thought. Emma.

What he was thinking was crazy. It had no basis in cold, hard sense. He had to ignore it.

169

Luckily there was so much medicine to concentrate on that he could hardly be where Emma was.

Luckily?

No. He wanted to be there. Of course he did.

But he had a life to lead. He had to get on with the life he'd chosen. The fact that a rotund little barrel of blazing energy had mobilised the town, sequestered the house, taken over his life...

She couldn't be allowed to make any difference at all.

Every night he dropped in briefly between house calls to get a briefing—a slick report on everything that had been achieved that day and a request for approval of what was planned for the next. It took ten minutes. He'd get home, Emma would be waiting for him, he'd take in the report and he'd leave again. Then he'd do house calls or go back to the hospital and catch up on paperwork or he'd visit Margaret.

He didn't return to the house until he was sure that Emma would be in bed, and he was gone at dawn.

They both knew why he didn't spend time in the house. Or he thought that maybe they both knew. He certainly knew himself.

She might well guess. Maybe she guessed.

Maybe he was being ridiculous.

But his house was being transformed.

'We're doing great,' Emma told him a week after she'd arrived, and he could only agree. It
wasn't just the children who were working. The
community had taken on this project as if it was a
way of preventing collective disintegration. The
school bus had come so close to sliding into the
sea and if it had, every one of these kids would be
dead. The townsfolk only had to look at Kyle's
parents to see how close they'd all come to their
own devastation.

'They should be doing something for Kyle's
parents,' he told Emma, but she shook her head.

'It's too direct. Kyle's parents need this project
as much as anyone. You know they all love you.'

'The hell they do.'

'That scares you,' she said thoughtfully, and he
felt his gut tighten in irritation. Or something. He
didn't know what. Unnerved, he grabbed his doctor's bag and turned to leave. He'd had his ten-
minute report.

'I have a house call to do,' he told her, and he
knew his voice was too brusque. It was almost
rude.

'You don't normally work eighteen hours a
day,' she said. They were standing in the newly
painted, beautifully scrubbed, fresh-smelling
kitchen. It was eight at night and he'd dropped in
really, really briefly. It was his nominal nightly

appearance before fleeing again. Fleeing from what, he didn't know.

He didn't normally work eighteen hours? 'I do,' he told her.

'Liar,' she said softly. 'I talked to Margaret. She says you're working like a madman. You're normally busy but not as busy as this.'

'Little she'd know. The bus crash has caused all sorts of repercussions.'

She raised her brows in polite incredulity. 'Who's your house call to, then?'

'Craig Hammond.'

'Is it urgent?' She cocked her head to one side. 'How urgent, Dev?'

'Craig's had pneumonia. I let him out of hospital on Thursday. I told him I'd check.'

'Has he called to say he's in trouble?'

He tried a glower. 'No.'

His glower didn't work. She was like a particularly persistent mosquito, still there no matter how hard he slapped. 'So you're planning to drop in on a Saturday night just to check that he's not dead. Does Craig live alone?'

'No, but…'

'But what?'

'Look, what the hell business is this of yours?'

'I'm not sure,' she said thoughtfully. 'I'm trying to figure it out.' She wiped her paint-stained hands on a rag. 'Can I come with you?'

'No!'

'Why not?'

'Why would you want to?'

'I'm a doctor,' she reminded him. 'I'm missing medicine.'

'You're supposed to be resting.' He eyed her stained hands with disapproval, trying to distract himself with medical need. If only he could think of her as a patient. 'You're not supposed to be painting.'

'I'm doing the neat little bits around the architraves,' she told him. She motioned to the said architraves. 'They're fun. Don't you think I'm doing a great job?'

'Yeah, but…'

There was a moment's silence. 'Yeah, but you'll get involved with me if you stay a moment longer,' she told him.

'I beg your pardon?'

'Like you're stuck being involved with the townsfolk. You're running scared.' She gave him a long, considering look. 'Of me. It's true, isn't it, Dev? You're scared of getting involved with me.'

'I'm not scared of getting involved with you. You're Corey's wife.'

'Corey's dead.'

There was a long, drawn-out silence at that. It continued far longer than was sensible. They were staring at each other over the table, and Emma wasn't giving up. Her eyes were defiant. Challenging.

Downright gorgeous.

'What the hell are you suggesting?' Dev demanded at last, and Emma gave a shaken laugh.

'I'm not sure. It's only… I looked at you then and thought, That's what it is. You're afraid of me.'

'Why would I be afraid of you?'

'Because of how we feel.'

'I don't—'

'Oh, Dev, cut it out,' she said tiredly, letting her gaze drop for a moment. Breaking the contact as if it was all suddenly too much. 'We both know what we're feeling. Like we want to jump each other right now.'

'Of all the—'

'Hey, I'm not suggesting we have an affair,' she told him. 'So you can get that look of shock and horror off your face right now.'

'It's not shock and horror.'

'Oh, yes, it is. Like I might indeed jump you.' She grinned, but her smile was strained. Tired. 'How could I dare?' she asked him. 'I couldn't in a million years.' She looked down at her bulge and she grimaced. 'Come to think of it, I'd probably end up squashing you.'

'You…'

'But this isn't about me and you,' she said softly, her smile fading. 'It's more than that. It's your whole dislike of involvement. That's from Corey, isn't it? He's dead. But he's holding you. You feel so darned responsible that you can't let go.' She hesitated and then she obviously decided she'd gone so far now, that there was no pulling back. 'Dev, there's no need for you to stay in this town. You can go.'

He stared at her, astounded. 'What are you talking about?'

'You heard me. There's no need for you to stay here, being a martyr. You can leave any time you want.'

'Don't be ridiculous. How can I possibly go? My mother…'

'Your mother will survive. She might even go to the States to visit you.'

'She wouldn't.'

'She might.'

'And this community?' He was angry now—really angry. How dared she stand there and say calmly that he could just walk away? The whole idea was mad. 'The community needs me.'

Her face stilled. 'They'll find someone else. Maybe a replacement's easier than you think.'

'That's a crazy statement,' he retorted. 'There are no doctors willing to work in such an isolated place as this.'

'I might.'

Her words took his breath away.

He couldn't think what to say next. The silence went on and on. *I might.* The words echoed around the kitchen, weirdly portentous.

'What do you mean?' he asked at last.

'I mean I might well stay here,' she told him, diffident and slightly unsure, but seemingly game for all that. 'For ever. I might even like it. And if I were to stay…that'd let you go back to your beloved job in the States.'

He shook his head, unable to believe what he was hearing. 'I don't— For heaven's sake, Emma, what on earth are you saying?'

'It's easy,' she told him. She plonked herself into a chair and poured herself a glass of red lemonade. She drank it slowly, staring over the rim of the glass at him. Thoughtful. Assessing. Taking her time to answer.

'What's easy?' he demanded at last, goaded beyond belief.

'Me taking over your conscience,' she told him. Then, as his confusion deepened, she tried to explain. 'Dev, you came back here because of tragedy. Your father was dead, Corey was dead, your mother was traumatised. The community was desperate for a doctor and your mother needed you. So you stayed. Now you see no escape. You're trapped with Corey's ghost and you can't get away. But me... I've been thinking... I kind of like Corey's ghost.'

'What the hell do you mean by that?'

'Corey was a lovely man,' she said softly. 'He saved my life, in more ways than one. He's given me my baby. I couldn't save him but I'll always be eternally grateful. And I've been thinking, one way of repaying that debt is to rescue his family.'

This was getting more ridiculous by the minute. 'I don't need rescuing.'

'You know, I'm very sure you do,' she told him. She set her glass down, stared at it for a moment as if she was wondering whether she needed another but finally appeared to decide against it. She looked doubtfully up at his face—and then she rose and came around to him. Face to face. Eighteen inches apart.

Far, far too close.

He had to concentrate on what she was saying. He couldn't concentrate on the fact that she was way too close for comfort.

He so wanted to reach out...

He didn't.

'Dev, you want to go back to the States,' she told him. 'Your work is important to you. And you could go. If I stay here... I think your mother's terrific. If I asked her, I bet she'd move in here like a shot and she'll help me bring up her grandchild. I'd take over the medicine in the town. Your mother would still have family. And you'd be left free. You could marry Margaret if you like. You could do anything that you want to do. The ghosts would be mine and I'd love them to bits. They wouldn't hurt me, Dev. They never could.'

Silence. He stared at her in stunned disbelief. If anyone could ever be said to have his jaw at his ankles, that was where his jaw was now.

'You're kidding,' he whispered.

'You think I'd kid about something as important as this?'

'What about Paul?'

She hesitated. She turned away and fiddled with her cordial glass for a bit and then she turned back to him again.

'I think we both know that that's not going to happen,' she told him slowly, as if she was considering each word. 'I've been thinking and thinking this week. Last night… Last night I told Paul I couldn't marry him, and we both know why.'

He drew in his breath. The night was spinning out of his control and he had no way of stopping it. 'Because of Corey?'

'Don't be obtuse. Dev, I thought I loved Corey three years ago when I was too sick to know what I was doing. I lost him for two years and then I saw him once more, seven months ago. He saved my life and he's fathered my child, but he's dead. How could this possibly be about Corey?'

'Then what…?'

She spread her hands, exasperated. 'Dev, I don't have any answers. I have no idea why I'm feeling like I'm feeling and it's totally inappropriate and of course you don't want it and that's OK, too. I understand. I'm not about to be another of your guilt trips. Another responsibility. I shouldn't have said anything but you did ask—about Paul—and you deserve the truth. So now you know.'

So now he knew. What?

He didn't have a clue what he knew.

Hell.

She just had to look at him, he thought savagely. She just had to look at him and…

He had to get out of here.

'Emma, this is pre-birth nerves or something,' he told her, edging slowly toward the door, like a man staring down the barrel of a loaded shotgun. She stared after him, still thoughtful, her eyes not leaving his face.

'It's not pre-birth nerves and you know it.'

'I need to go.'

'Of course you do.' She even managed a smile. 'I hope Craig enjoys having his Saturday night television interrupted by an unnecessary doctor's visit.

'It's necessary.'

'Is it?' Her brows rose. 'I met Craig in hospital. His pneumonia wasn't severe and it resolved fast with antibiotics. He's more than capable of lifting the phone if his symptoms recur. Which they won't. So why are you running, Dev?'

'I'm not running.'

'Tomorrow the kids will be here,' she said, seemingly veering off on a tangent. 'It's Sunday. We've got such plans. You know, they—the kids and their parents—would all be thrilled to bits if you came and helped.'

'I can't.'

'Of course you can't.' Her face stilled. There was even a hint of reproof there now. 'All these imperatives.'

'Emma…'

'I know.' She spread her hands again, this time in frustration. 'It's none of my business.' She sighed. 'And of course you're right. I'm none of your my business. Why you'd look twice at a woman loaded with your brother's child I can't imagine. Maybe it's all my imagination—this frisson between us. But it has made me break things off with Paul. It has made me see that if I can't have everything, then… I don't want second best. And meanwhile… What I'm offering is serious, Dev. I have no ties anywhere now. I love this place. I love your mother and she loves the fact that I'm having Corey's baby. So if you indeed want to take yourself back to America…'

'I do. I mean...I'd like to.' He wasn't making sense. Nothing was making sense. Would he like to? Last week he had been sure of it. Now...

Of course he'd like to.

'There you are, then,' she was saying. 'It's a perfect solution.'

'Just like that?'

'Just like that.'

He stared at her for a few moments longer. She gazed calmly back, as if what she was saying made all the sense in the world.

'You'll think differently in the morning.'

'Maybe I will.' She nodded, thoughtful. 'Who can tell? So you don't think you ought to sign me up now?'

'No!'

'And you're leaving to do your house call. But you'll come back and help the kids tomorrow?' Her tone was suddenly almost pleading. 'Dev, they'd love it.'

'I...'

'Please, Dev. The entire town will be here. The mums are putting on a barbecue on the beach. It'll be such fun.'

'Life's not supposed to be fun,' he snapped, and she smiled as if he'd said something ridiculous.

'Hey, that's where you're wrong, Dev,' she told him. 'It's a stupid thing to say. I spent a childhood of no fun. Life's slapped me hard but I don't intend to stay meekly being slapped over and over again. From now on I take life—I take fun—where I can find it. Which is why I'm offering what I'm offering. I think it'd be great to stay here. Even if you and I can't sort out…what seems to be between us, then your ghosts and I intend to have a very good time indeed. With or without you.'

What had she done?

Emma lay in bed and stared at the shafts of moonlight washing over her ceiling. Outside the sea was a soft hushed murmur and an owl was calling in eerie hooting calls over the bay.

This was the best place to raise a kid. It felt like home. She'd never felt like this about a place before.

How much of that was the way she'd fallen for Dev?

She was really so confused.

'I shouldn't have said anything to him,' she whispered to the dark. 'Talk about wearing your heart on your sleeve. It was so unfair. You practically told the man you'd fallen in love with him.

'Well, you have.

'You thought you were in love with Corey.

'I fell in love with Corey's smile. That was all I knew. It was all I could see. And his kindness. I was so sick. But with Dev…it's as if here's the smile, here's the kindness, but so much more.

'What exactly?

'I don't know.'

It was just as well Dev was still out, doing his rounds, ministering to the sick whether they needed it or not, playing with Margaret...

Not a good thought.

Regardless, it was just as well he was away, as her whispers had become a wail. 'I don't know why I've fallen in love with him,' she told the dark. 'I only know my life was nicely on track. Here's Paul being so patient and so kind, and waiting for me for all this time—and I just have to look into Dev's eyes and know that nothing's ever going to work with Paul.

'It's romantic nonsense.

'Probably,' she admitted. 'And maybe Dev's sensible enough to see it. He's gone back to Margaret. But at least what's happening does affirm what I want to do. I do want to stay here. I want to raise Corey's baby here.

'With Dev.

'Without Dev,' she said resolutely. 'He'll be gone. You've given him an out. He can leave for America just as soon as you're fit to take over his medical practice.

'But you hope he won't.

'What I hope has nothing to do with it. My hopes...they're perfectly ridiculous.' She hauled her sheet up to her nose and stared up at her newly painted ceiling. 'What I hope… What I hope is a stupid dream. But, oh, it's a dream worth dreaming.'

She closed her eyes determinedly. 'OK. Let's dream. Let's dream as hard as we can. But for heaven's sake, remember the script when you wake up, so you can play it out in real life. Or you can try.'

Contrary to what Emma believed, Dev wasn't at Margaret's. Neither was he interrupting his patient's television viewing.

He'd driven out the gate. He'd stopped and then he'd walked back. Down to the cove. Along the beach.

Now he sat on the rocky headland overlooking the bay, gazing out over the moonlit sea. And like, Emma, he started talking to himself.

'I can leave.

'Yeah?

'Yeah. You can. It's what you want. You can take up where you left off. She's let you off the hook.

'I sort of like…

'What? Being here?

'Things have changed.

'What's changed?' He was talking to the sea, to the dark, to the glossy blue swimmer crabs feeding on the low tide detritus on rocks at his feet.

'I don't know what's changed.

'You do know what's changed. Everything. Emma's changed everything.

'Emma is Corey's.

'Corey's dead.'

He stirred uneasily. 'So get on with it,' he told himself. 'Move. Emma's offered you a way out. The way you're feeling about Emma...it's all tied up with how you feel about Corey. Would you still want Emma if she wasn't Corey's widow?

'So you do admit you want her?

'No. Yes!' He glared at a particularly large crab and the crab stopped its pincer-to-mouth movements and appeared to glare right back.

'How's your love life?' he asked, and the crab hesitated and then went straight back to eating.

'You're telling me to get on with it. Take up Emma's offer? Leave?

'That's sensible.'

Could he?

Margaret would come with him, he thought. Of course she would. She'd felt as trapped as he was in this place. She'd gone to the city to do basic nursing training but had returned to care for her elderly parents. Her father had died two years ago, and her mother had followed last month. She was free to go. She was only staying here because of Dev.

Hell.

He hadn't wanted this.

'So what do you want?

'A simple life. No complications.

'Not Emma?

'No!' It was a shout into the empty night, and the crab scuttled sideways in fright.

'Sorry, mate,' Dev said. He stood and raked one hand through his hair, staring out over the sea, trying to make his tired mind think.

'I'll sleep at Mum's.

'Right. And tomorrow?

'I'll sleep at Mum's tonight. I'll go to this damned working bee tomorrow. For a while.

'And after that?

'Who knows? I sure as hell don't. I wish she'd never come.

'Do you?

'I don't have a clue. Not a single clue. Not a one.'

CHAPTER EIGHT

HE MUST have slept at Margaret's.

Emma had slept fitfully and she was sure she would have heard if Dev's car had returned. It hadn't. At dawn she woke and walked for half an hour on the beach, trying not to look at the empty place where Dev usually parked his car.

He'd slept at Margaret's.

What was she doing, wearing her heart on her sleeve like a silly teenager?

She sat on the beach and stared at the sea. A pod of dolphins surfed into the cove, their sleek, silver-black bodies streamlined and agile as they gloried in the sun and surf and the morning.

He'd slept at Margaret's.

You're a dope, she told herself. She pushed herself to her feet and tried not to think about crying. She had no business crying. This was the most glorious place in the world. She had dolphins watching her. In an hour she'd have the world's biggest working bee—otherwise known as a party—starting right here.

He'd slept at Margaret's.

'Get on with it,' she told herself. She stared out at the dolphins and then she laid a hand on her tummy. 'You have everything in the world to be thankful for. Stop wanting the unobtainable.

'How can I stop wanting?'

He'd slept at Margaret's.

The ambulance arrived to collect Beryl Cootes at ten a.m. Beryl was due to have valve replacement surgery the next day in Brisbane, so the ambulance service had combined two jobs into one run: bringing Colin Jeffries home and collecting Beryl. Suzy and Jodie needed a while longer in Brisbane but Colin was fine to return.

Dev was waiting. Of course Dev was waiting. He'd been at the hospital since dawn, he'd run out of work and Colin's return was a blessing. He'd have to work through his admission and he didn't have to think about the working bee that was happening without him.

Besides, he liked Colin. Colin's wife had died young and his only daughter had married a US marine, but Colin never seemed to be lonely. The mild-mannered, middle-aged teacher loved Karington. He was active in the preservation of the national park. He loved his small students and they, in turn, loved him.

They might love him even more now, Dev thought as he checked him out. Nothing like a long scar right down the side of a face to make a man look interesting.

'I should get an eye-patch and do the whole pirate thing,' Colin told him. 'Dev, let me go home. I've had enough of hospitals.'

'You're not going home until your stitches are out and I'm sure your blood's OK,' Dev told him. Colin had suffered deep-vein thrombosis two years back and was on anticoagulants—which was one of the reasons he'd bled so much at the crash. He'd been taken off the heparin, but now he had to be gradually reintroduced to it. 'Your shoulder's still useless and you can't change your own dressing. Stay here and let us look after you. And you're damned lucky you aren't doing the whole pirate bit. If that cut had been an inch to the right...'

'Yeah, I'd have been stuffed,' Colin said. 'As it was, they're telling me it was some lady doctor and one of my kids who saved me. Katy?'

'Yeah, Katy.' Dev refused to let himself dwell on the 'some lady doctor' thing. 'Katy's a great kid.'

'They've all sent me cards,' Colin told him. 'And they're telling me they've started a project in memory of Kyle. Out at your place? I wish I could be there.'

'It's good.'

'This lady doctor is in charge?'

So much for not talking about her. 'Emma. Her name's Emma.'

'Yeah, Emma. She's living with you?'

'I... Yeah. She's Corey's widow. You know, this scar is going to fade. It's looking angry now but they've done a great job with the stitching. It'll just be a hairline.'

But Colin wasn't interested in his scar. 'Corey's widow.' He stared up from the pillows of the bed he'd just been moved to. 'That's a damned thing. Did you know Corey had been married?'

'Not until the bus crash. First I knew of her was when I fell over her. She was almost unconscious.'

'I'll bet you were knocked sideways.'

'Yeah.' He thought about it. 'Yeah, maybe I was.'

'Is she nice?'

'Um.' Dev thought about it. Or tried to think about it. 'Yeah, she's very nice. Can I give you some pain relief?'

'In a minute. I need to think this through.'

'There's nothing to think about. Is your shoulder hurting?'

'Only when I laugh, and I'm not laughing now.' Colin had come to Karington as a young teacher some thirty years before. He'd taught both Corey and Dev. He knew everything about everyone in this town—except this. 'Emma.' He said the name slowly, considering. 'I vaguely remember her from the crash. She was pregnant?'

'Yes. Look, Colin, you really need to rest.'

'Corey's child?'

'Yes.'

'Well, I'll be damned. I bet Lorna is tickled pink.'

'My mother's pretty happy,' Dev admitted.

'And she's a doctor.'

'Yes.'

Colin's eyes narrowed. 'She hasn't come to stay?'

'I don't know.'

'You mean she might?'

'She says she'd like to.' The words sounded as if they had been dragged out of Dev and Colin's eyes narrowed still further—and then stopped narrowing as the motion pulled his stitched face and hurt. He schooled his face into impassivity but then went right on.

'Hell, Dev, that means...'

'That I can go,' Dev said roughly. 'I know. Colin, give me a minute to check your chart.'

'You know as well as I do what it'll say. They started the heparin again yesterday so in a few days I should be back to normal. Otherwise I'm fine. I'm back to normal now. I can go home.'

'You're staying here,' Dev growled. 'Meanwhile, shut up and let me study the chart.'

'Why don't you want to talk about Emma?'

'I'm happy to talk about Emma. But I'm busy.'

'Yeah?' Colin eyed his ex-student with mild interest. 'It's Sunday morning. What have you got on after me?'

'Nothing. I mean...'

'So you're heading out to this working bee the kids are at?'

'No, I...'

'Because of Emma.'

'She's Corey's widow,' Dev said desperately, and Colin's eyes narrowed all over again. He winced but this apparently was important. His eyes kept right on narrowing.

'Well, well.'

'There's no well, well about it.'

'You're in love with her.'

Oh, great. 'Don't be ridiculous.' He set down Colin's notes with a sharp slap on the bedside tray. 'How can I be in love with Corey's widow? And what about Margaret?'

'What about Margaret?' Colin asked thoughtfully. 'Hell, Dev, you're supposed to have been in love with Margaret for the last couple of years, yet I haven't seen a sign of it in the pair of you. Affection, yes. Love, no.'

'Colin, for—'

'For nothing.' Colin ventured a careful smile. 'Get out of here and go to the working bee.'

'Will you butt out?'

'Nope,' Colin said cheerfully. He even managed a grin, despite his stitches. 'Well, well. I thought I might be bored stupid for the rest of the school holidays. And here I am not bored at all. Not even a little bit. Are you sure I can't get up and go out and meet this Emma?'

'No!'

'Well, you go for me, then,' Colin said. 'If I write out a list of twenty questions, can you get them answered for me? Just pretend it's home-work.'

It was almost lunchtime. The property was a hive of activity—a swarm of people transforming the place into something she could barely recognise.

Everyone was there except Dev.

'It's damned near going to be a botanical garden after we finish with it.' Kyle's dad was by Emma's side, surveying his remaining kids' work with quiet satisfaction. 'You know, every time we drive past this place in the future we're going to look at it and say it's Kyle's garden.'

'I hope you do.' Lorna was offering lemonade to anyone who looked in the least bit hot. 'And it's Corey's garden as well. Kyle and Corey.' She smiled, a gentle smile that had been missing from her face for far too long. 'You know, I'm sure they're here watching us be here,' she murmured. 'Corey and Kyle. Somewhere.'

'Ghosts are great,' Emma said softly, looking around her in quiet satisfaction at all they'd achieved. 'They'll love it here. What better place to haunt?'

'I thought…when we're finished maybe we can set up a seat with Kyle's name on it.' Graham Connor looked a bit uncomfortable about suggesting such a thing but he kept on. The big man dug his hands deep into his pockets and glowered, obviously fighting to stop tears welling from behind his eyes. 'The missus and I thought…up on the headland. Just beyond the boundaries of this place but where we can sit and look over this and the cove. We can see everything there. Where the bus crashed. This garden where the kids worked to remember him. The cove. We can just go and sit there…whenever.'

'I think that's a lovely idea,' Lorna said warmly. 'What about if I build another seat on the opposite side of the cove for Corey?'

'That'd be wonderful,' Emma said in a voice that was none too steady.

She excused herself and left the two parents making plans.

This was good. Wasn't it?

Of course it was good. She moved among the kids and listened to them bossing each other about and laughing and talking. Kyle's garden. Corey's garden.

Ghosts.

'Ghosts are for the past,' she whispered. 'What about the future?'

Could she live here? Without Dev?

'Oh, for heaven's sake, move on,' she told herself. 'You're being dumb.'

'Miss?'

She turned, grateful for any the distraction from her jumbled thoughts. Jemima Reynolds was calling. Jemima and Katy had been painting the veranda rail when last she'd seen them—two gloriously happy little girls with more paint on their persons than on the handrails. 'Hi, Jem.' She smiled. 'Problem?'

There obviously was a problem.

'Katy said… Katy said could I come and get you,' Jem's voice was quavering in distress. 'Our paint tin fell off the veranda and hit Katy's side. It made her fall over. I didn't think it hit her very hard but Katy's gone all white. She's crying and crying. She wouldn't let me tell anyone else except you. Can you come?'

Katy was in trouble.

The quiet kids were the ones to look at first. Katy was definitely quiet. She definitely needed attention. Now.

When Emma reached her she'd rolled out of sight of the veranda under a fiery red callistemon, curling into a ball of whimpering distress. When Emma reached in to touch her, she gasped and pulled back.

Emma's heart lurched. What on earth...?

'Don't...don't...'

Thoroughly alarmed now, Emma crawled in under the foliage where Katy lay like a wounded wild creature. 'It's OK, Katy,' she said softly. In seconds she'd switched into medical mode, every sense working on overload. 'It's me. You know I'm a doctor. Let me help you. Where does it hurt?'

'M-my side.' The little girl's breath was coming in short, shallow gasps that spoke of real pain. Intolerable pain. Her eyes behind her thick glasses were wide with terror.

She was white. Bloodless. Sweaty.

Ten minutes ago she'd been fine.

Emma's fingers reached for the side of her neck, searching for a pulse. What she found was hardly reassuring. It was fast, irregular and thready.

She was in shock, Emma thought incredulously. Why?

'What happened?' She turned to Jemima. 'Did the paint tin land right on her? Was it a big tin?'

'It's only little.' Jem was almost as pale as Katy. 'It slid off the veranda and it just sort of brushed her. But I think she was scared it had the lid off. She jumped back and fell over. She...she got up and said, ''Lucky it had the lid on.'' Then...then she grabbed her side and she started to cry. And then she started...not crying. Sort of, I dunno...moaning. She crawled under the bush and said she wanted to be sick.'

'Well done, Jem,' Emma told her. 'You described that really well. Katy, you need to tell me where it hurts.'

Emma's fingers were on Katy's side, working her way gently up her body. Her hands were scarcely a feather touch. Watching Katy's face as she worked.

Nothing in the groin. Further. Up the left side. To the right.

Rigidity. Pain. Excruciating pain.

Katy's eyes said it all.

And Emma's heart sank. The lovely morning was over and the terror of the last few days was right back with them.

The diagnosis was screaming at her. Upper right quadrant pain. Sudden onset after only minor trauma. Severe shock, weak pulse, sweaty. There must be internal bleeding to account for this amount of shock. Massive internal bleeding.

Bus crash a week ago.

Spleen. Ruptured spleen. It had to be.

Dear God.

'Katy…'

'I…can't…' Katy whispered, and her eyes rolled.

She was losing consciousness. Already! Dear God.

'Jemima, find the nearest grown-up,' Emma said, trying to sound calm. 'Run. Tell them I need a car. I need someone to ring Dr O'Halloran. Yell that to everyone. Tell someone to ring Dr O'Halloran and bring the phone to me. Fast.'

Jemima took one swift look at her friend. She gulped and choked on a sob—and she fled.

Jemima was one dependable little girl. A minute later Emma had half a dozen concerned adults around her feet. She could only see their feet. She wasn't moving Katy out from under her bush until she had a car to move her to.

There was a babble of concern above her but there was no time to allay their fears. There was no way she could.

'Is someone phoning Dev?' She was rolling Katy gently to her side to try and make breathing easier. Damn, why didn't she have a doctor's bag? What was the use of being a doctor when she didn't have equipment?

She wanted plasma expander and oxygen. Now.

'Dialling,' someone told her.

'Who's got the nearest car?'

'Me.' It was Graham Connor, Kyle's dad. 'What the hell…?'

'Bring it up here. Close. Don't worry what you squash in the garden, just get it close. There's no time for an ambulance. Where are Katy's parents?'

'They're not here.' It was Lorna, confused, distressed. 'I'll get someone to ring them. Emma, what's going on?'

'Dev's on the line.' Someone was bending, handing Emma a cellphone. She didn't answer Lorna but grabbed the phone. Her spare hand stayed on Katy's neck, willing the thready pulse to continue.

'Dev?'

'What is it, Emma?'

He was there. His deep voice grounded her, pushing away panic. A little. Panic was the last thing that was needed here, she told herself, and somehow the sound of his voice helped her to revert to the professional she had to be.

'It's Katy,' she told him. Heck, she didn't even know Katy's surname. 'Katy who helped us at the bus crash. Dev, there was a trivial accident—a paint pot hit Katy's side and she fell over. It shouldn't have caused injury. But she's collapsed. It's looking like there's internal bleeding—a lot of internal bleeding. Everything's pointing to a ruptured spleen. She's losing ground fast.'

'Katy.' There was a split second's silence while he figured out who she was talking about—and then assimilated the enormity of what they were facing. She could hear his mind racing.

A ruptured spleen. A nightmare scenario.

The violence of the bus crash must have caused a tear. Impossible to diagnose. Katy had been checked, Emma knew. There'd been what had seemed minor bruising—all the kids had bruising—but there hadn't even been a broken rib to explain this.

But it must have torn all the same. Somehow it hadn't bled enough to cause problems, just remained *in situ*, like a lethal time bomb. If Katy had stayed immobile for weeks—or if she'd been lucky—the thing might have cured itself. But now... The paint tin had fallen, she'd jerked backward and tumbled. The split must have ruptured completely.

The internal bleeding would be horrendous. Life-threatening. Fatal?

'Where are you?' she demanded of Dev. Please, God, let him be at the hospital.

'At the hospital. We can do a CT scan—'

'There's no time for scans.'

'That bad?'

'Worse.'

He trusted her. She heard his sharp intake of breath and she heard him regroup.

'Right. Get her in here as fast as you safely can. I'll have Theatre ready to go the minute you arrive. You can do the anaesthetic?'

'Is there an anaesthetist available?'

'No.' Harsh. Definite.

'Then of course.' Of course? She wasn't an anaesthetist but she could manage. Probably. If they were in time.

She knew the rules of anaesthetics. She knew the basics. She was all Katy had.

Please, let it be enough.

'Don't take any chances on the way in,' Dev snapped. 'But get here as fast as you can. I'll be waiting.'

Karington hospital might be a remote bush-nursing hospital in the middle of nowhere, but the efficiency of the staff could put city hospitals to shame. Margaret was at the doors of the emergency room when they arrived. An orderly—Matt, a kid who looked not much older than Katy—had a stretcher waiting, and he had the car's back door hauled open before they had completely stopped.

'Dev's in Theatre,' Margaret said as she reached in to see what they were facing. 'He's scrubbing.' She looked down at Katy's deathly pale face and her own face puckered in distress. 'Oh, my dear.'

But there was no time for distress and Margaret knew it.

'Oxygen, fast,' Emma snapped. Matt had it ready. Margaret handed Emma the mask, then moved back to let Matt access to the little girl and she turned to ready an IV line.

'Minimal movement, Matt,' Emma warned as she fitted the mask. 'Be careful.'

Katy was no longer conscious.

She looked dreadful, Emma thought as she helped Matt manoeuvre Katy out of the car. Close to death. Katy's glasses fell aside and landed on the floor of the car, and there was no time to retrieve them.

Please, God, may she need them again.

She was on the stretcher now. Emma was out of the car herself and the crash cart was under her hand almost as her feet hit the ground. Margaret handed a swab and a syringe to Emma, then grabbed the child's shirt cuff and ripped from wrist to shoulder.

'I need plasma expander,' Emma snapped. She was wearing gum boots—black rubber rain boots—and her crazy red maternity smock, and she didn't feel in the least like a doctor, but she was very much a doctor and that was how Margaret was treating her. Emma had been here last as a patient but she now needed be a professional—and a good one. 'And I need blood for cross-matching.'

'There's plasma expander here.' Margaret was manoeuvring a stand at her elbow, the first bag already hung, the line ready, waiting for Emma to find a vein.

Emma found a vein.

Thank God she was a paediatrician. Locating veins in children could be notoriously difficult, but Emma had inserted a thousand.

They were moving fast. The stretcher trolley was already rolling inside the entrance. Matt might be young but he was good. The IV was inserted on the move. The trolley was inside the door before the drip started to flow.

Margaret had a blood-pressure cuff on now, linked to an electronic monitor. She read the initial results and gasped. 'My God.'

'Don't even think about it,' Emma ordered. She was kicking off her gumboots as they moved. There was no time for her to change into theatre gear but maybe the muddy boots could go. Which left her in socks. She wasn't thinking about socks. 'Let's just get in there and stop the bleeding.'

Down the long corridor. Precious seconds spent turning corners. Katy was deeply unconscious. She'd be losing blood supply to the brain. Please…

The doors to Theatre swung open.

Dev was ready.

Emma blinked at the sudden glare of the theatre lights. At the waiting tableau, Dev was gowned and gloved and masked. There were two more nurses working frantically, preparing equipment.

Dev had moved with a speed that was unbelievable.

But there was no time for reflection on how fast they were moving. They had to keep going. The trolley was pushed against the table and swift, capable hands were lifting Katy across, careful not to disturb the flow of oxygen, careful of the IV line. Scissors were slicing clothes, lifting them clear, draping…

'You're sure?' Dev snapped, and Emma knew what he was asking.

'Upper right quadrant pain with shock after light trauma. Massive loss of blood pressure. Loss of consciousness. Dev, we need to assume…'

He asked no more questions. 'Get that anaesthetic in,' Dev snapped. 'Light anaesthetic, Emma. As light as you can.'

The anaesthetic trolley was beside her.

Right.

Emma took a deep breath, and then she steadied. She paused for just a moment. This might be an emergency—it was an emergency—but she wasn't an anaesthetist. She needed to make absolutely sure that she was doing the right thing.

'Let me run this past you.' She figured it out in her head and then repeated the anaesthetic dosage to Dev, knowing he'd understand her uncertainty.

He knew she was a paediatrician who spent very little time in Theatre. He'd know what was being asked of her now was a conjuring up of training that had taken place a long time ago. 'Can you confirm dosage or do I need to set up a link with a paediatric anaesthetist?'

'There's no need,' he told her. 'That's good.'

All she could see of Dev was his eyes, but she looked up and his eyes were on hers.

They were asking a question. They were demanding a response.

They were steadying her, holding her. You can do this, he was saying.

He could do this as well.

'We read the same training manual Emma,' he told her. 'And I've spent half my training in paediatric surgery. I concur.'

'Blood pressure's still dropping,' Margaret warned. 'Dev, we're going to lose her.'

'We're not going to lose her,' Dev said quietly, calmly, as if he were about to perform a simple operation on an ingrown toenail. He was watching Emma administer the anaesthetic but he kept a wary eye on the monitors. 'We have a competent anaesthetist and a competent surgeon and three exceedingly competent nurses. What else do we need?'

There was a tiny laugh—almost hysterical—from one of the nurses, but his words had their effect. As a team, they steadied.

Emma's syringe found its mark and the anaesthetic flowed through. A nurse was waiting with what she needed. Emma took the intubation tube from the nurse. As the muscles relaxed, she lifted Katy's chin and slid the tube home.

The machine took over Katy's breathing.

Over to Dev.

'Go,' she said.

They went.

Afterwards, when Emma thought about the operation they performed that morning, she'd shake her head in disbelief.

Dev worked swiftly with his scalpel, exposing the damage they'd suspected. As their suspicions were confirmed, Emma took one look and thought Dev didn't have time for anything. So much blood... He had to locate the spleen, cut and seal its attachments to other organs and lift it from the wound. All behind the ribs. It'd take time they didn't have.

Surely Katy would die under his hands.

But no. Dev's fingers worked with a speed she couldn't believe. Searching, clamping, swabbing...

Emma was working desperately herself. The child's breathing was so fragile. How much damage had been done already?

Oxygen to maximum. Please…

She glanced back to what Dev was doing. She expected the spleen to emerge, lifted free.

It didn't happen.

'The lower pole's dusky,' he muttered, talking to himself. 'Capsular disruption. Hell, it's solidly split. But the upper…'

His fingers were steady, clever, intuitive. Where another surgeon would have been searching desperately for blood vessels, attachments to other organs, he seemed to know instinctively where everything was located.

His eyes, the only thing that could be seen under his theatre gear, were fierce with concentration.

'I think…'

'What are you doing?' Emma's voice was a gasp.

'A partial splenectomy. Maybe.' Dev's voice was steady. His eyes flicked fleetingly to the monitor. 'I think… I have it now. If I can't get a seal then I'll back off and take the whole thing out. But I'm sure… I think I'm sure…'

Emma's eyes were back on the monitor, seeing what Dev was seeing. 'More blood,' she snapped. 'Get another unit ready, Margaret.'

'Just lucky she's O-positive,' Margaret said grimly, already turning to find what was needed.

'I want my superglue,' Dev muttered. 'David…'

'Coming.' The nurse was handing Dev something that Emma didn't understand.

'Superglue?' Emma was concentrating fiercely on the child's fragile breathing, on her increasingly threatened vital signs, but she had room to wonder out loud. She wasn't asking Dev, though. No one was disturbing the intensity that was all that lay between life and death. She was asking the room in general. 'What's superglue?'

'Human fibrin glue.' Margaret even managed a smile, but her eyes didn't leave Dev's fingers. Every one of the nurses was anticipating urgent need from the two doctors. 'It's something new. Dev brought it from the States.'

'Used a lot in kids with tumours,' Dev said to no one in particular, his fingers still working. 'Brilliant stuff. If I have to be here, then I'm damned if I'll work with second-rate materials. Thromboplastic is state-of-the-art sealant.'

Silence. The soft beep of the monitor, the whistle of Katy's breath and the hum of the air-conditioner were the only noises. The tension was palpable. *Please.*

Dev was racing against time. Racing…

'Blood pressure?'

'Seventy on forty-five.'

'It's coming up.' Dev glanced. It was a fleeting second of consideration—gamble or not—and then a decision. 'Partial.'

More silence. The tension was unbearable.

'Mesh…'

At least Emma had heard of thrombostatic mesh, though she'd never seen it used as he was using it here. He'd lifted the damaged part of the spleen free, he'd sealed the remaining undamaged portion of spleen with his 'glue' and now he was wrapping the remaining spleen in mesh. Its role was to form a compression—to keep the spleen under the same pressure it had been under when whole. The mesh was made to dissolve in time, letting what was left of the spleen resume its function.

In the future… In Katy's future.

She might make it, Emma thought. Dear God, she might.

Her eyes were glued to the monitor.

Blood pressure was still rising.

This man was brilliant, Emma thought. Or a gambling fool.

She glanced at his fingers and she cut one choice off her list of two.

Dev was no fool. He'd looked at the damage, he'd decided he could do this and he'd gone for it. If it worked—as it now looked like it might well work—Katy would avoid a lifetime without a spleen. That meant a lifetime without the antibiotics and inoculations and monitoring for infections that full loss of spleen automatically implied. The part of the spleen Dev had saved would take over full function.

Please...

'We have full seal,' Dev said at last, and only now could Emma hear tension enter his voice. And fear? 'Em...'

'Blood pressure's still on the way up.'

'I'm closing.'

'Oh, God, have we done it?' Margaret whispered.

Silence.

The little girl's breathing was a harsh, whistling gasp through the intubation tube. Katy's small face, absurdly young, seemed totally defenceless without those crazy glasses.

'If she gets through this I'm going to buy her contact lenses,' Emma said, a trifle defiantly, and there was a crack of laughter from the young male nurse, David. The laughter was harsh with strain but it was laughter for all that.

'That's our Dr Em for you. What would we do without you? What did we do without you? A doctor who arrives at her operations wearing red tents and gumboots, who prescribes contact lenses for her small patients and who orders bright yellow Mini Coopers...'

'Hey!' Emma tried to sound indignant—and failed. She managed a smile. David was trying to break the tension with laughter. She recognised the attempt and appreciated it, but it wasn't working. This tension was unbreakable. They were all fiercely watching Katy's face. If she'd lost too much blood…

How much damage had been done to her brain?

'Can you reverse, Em?' Dev said, and the tension increased by about a thousand per cent. They all knew what this meant.

They'd given Katy the anaesthetic when she had been unconscious. Would she wake?

Please.

Emma slipped the reversal home. She took a deep breath.

'You've ordered a Mini?' Dev asked, and she shot him a look that was half defiant, half plain terrified. Then she went back to looking at Katy's face.

Please.

'The hire car company said I was a bad risk,' she managed. If they didn't talk of something else they'd go nuts. They were going nuts anyway. 'David's father's a car dealer in Brisbane so he's arranged it for me.'

'There's a yellow and black Mini Cooper S arriving this weekend for our Dr Em,' David said.

'Will our Dr Em fit behind the wheel?' Dev asked.

There was general laughter, horribly strained. Self-conscious. Trying far too hard.

Emma tried, but she couldn't manage to join in. She was watching Katy's face. Every ounce of her being was absorbed in Katy's face.

Dev was watching her.

She glanced up and met his eyes.

And for that tiny fraction of time their gazes held. And she saw...

Terror, she thought dully. She recognised Dev's fear for his little patient, but in that instant she also recognised that part of his fear was for her. He knew how much she was involved here. How much she wanted this.

He...loved her? In that instant of fleeting communication the barriers were suddenly down. Gone. Dissolved into nothing. She'd seen a truth behind his eyes that he was trying desperately to keep hidden.

He cared. What she felt... It wasn't one way. She'd known it couldn't be—this feeling that was so strong—and here was confirmation. That glance had been a linking of two halves. She knew what was in his mind—in his heart.

He was part of her. He was...her soul?

She was back watching Katy again but, damn, her eyes were blinking back tears. How could she cry? She couldn't cry. Not here. Not now.

Not ever.

'Come on, Katy,' she whispered. 'You can do this. Dr O'Halloran's used his wonderful human fibrin glue on you. Don't let it be for nothing.'

'Em…'

Dev said her name. It was a whisper. She didn't look up but she heard and she knew what it was.

Confirmation. Terror. Unification. They might as well be one, because that was what was happening here.

He was hers. Her Dev.

'Come on, Katy. Please. Please.' How professional was this? She didn't care. 'Come on, Katy. Katy…'

There was a rasping, jerking cough. The reversal of the relaxant anaesthetic. Katy's own breathing was recommencing.

Emma's fingers were lifting the intubation tube free. She was having trouble holding her fingers steady.

Dev's hands were still adjusting dressings. Taping them in place. There was no tremor in his fingers but there was definitely a tremor behind his eyes.

The dressing was being performed almost blind. His eyes were watching Katy. Everyone in the room was watching Katy.

The minutes ticked on.

And on.

The child's eyes opened.

Unseeing? Dear God.

Wait. It'd take time for her to resurface. Please. Wait.

'Katy?'

Nothing.

But maybe...just maybe there was a focussing. She couldn't bear to wait any longer.

'Katy, you've hurt your side.' Emma stooped so that Katy could see her face. If she could see. *Please.* 'The paint pot hit you and made something inside you bleed. We've taken you to hospital and we've stitched it up. You're OK. You're OK, Katy.'

Nothing. No response.

Dear God, please.

But something was changing. Katy's eyes were definitely focussing now, struggling through the mist of drugs and pain and terror.

Seeing Emma.

'Em.' It was a thread of a whisper, maybe imagined.

Not imagined.

'I'm here.' Emma lifted Katy's hand and held, hard. 'Your mum and dad are here, too, waiting for you to wake up.'

'Jem… Jem and I think that Kyle would want the veranda to be yellow,' Katy whispered. 'Tell Jem… Tell Jem not to finish without me.'

She closed her eyes, and retreated back into oblivion.

CHAPTER NINE

SHE was OK.

Katy was unbelievably, miraculously, wonder-fully fine. She roused again, enough to greet her tearful and near-hysterical parents, she was even heard to soothe them, and then she drifted into natural sleep. Her body would take time to recover but recover it would, with enough spleen left so there should be no long-term consequences.

Emma let Dev talk to Katy's parents. As soon as she was sure that Katy's breathing was stable, that consciousness was miraculously restored, she walked into the little dressing room beside Theatre and sat down. Hard.

She didn't move.

She coped with trauma. So what? she asked fiercely, trying to control the tremors that were running through her body. Coping with what had just happened was what she was trained to do. She'd faced life-and-death situations in her normal work so many times.

This was different.

This was Katy.

She belonged here, she thought as she sat and stared unseeingly at the linoleum floor of the washroom. More and more she knew that this was where she belonged. She'd come out here to meet Corey's family and she'd fallen in love.

She'd fallen in love with a community.

She'd fallen in love with Dev.

Which came first, the chicken or the egg? Who knew? All she knew was that for all her life she'd been rootless, drifting, unsure. Yet here the sensation of belonging was overwhelming. Her fear for Katy was a terror that part of this little community she loved would be destroyed.

How could she leave?

What she was thinking was nonsensical—crazy—without any sort of logical justification at all. Yet as she sat and stared at her shaking hands, she knew that the offer she'd made Dev would hold good no matter what he decided to do.

She'd stay here. It was her home. And if that offer set Dev free…well, she'd manage. Somehow.

The door opened and it was Dev.

'Emma.'

'Dev.' Her voice trailed off. His face was grey with exhaustion, and she so wanted to rise, to walk into his arms, to melt into the place where she belonged.

She didn't belong there, she told herself fiercely. No matter how linked they were, there were things that couldn't be altered. She was a woman who was heavy with his brother's child. For Dev to move past that might well be impossible. How could she ask it of him? It wasn't even fair.

'I can't believe you did that,' she murmured, staring at the linoleum again.

'I can't believe I did it either.' He started untying the strings of his mask, and again she had that urge to go to him. To help. To hold.

She couldn't. She mustn't. She had no right. If he couldn't see it—if he didn't want it—she had no right to intrude on his personal space.

'It was a risk,' she whispered, and he glanced down at her. He made a move toward her—and then drew back as if he'd just reminded himself who she was. Reminded himself to be professional.

'Not taking the entire spleen wasn't such a risk,' he told her. 'I've done that operation in kids with tumours. I didn't put Katy at any more risk than she already was. I don't believe she lost any more blood than if I'd done an entire splenectomy.

'And you had the equipment to do it.' She was speaking in a harsh whisper. He cast another uncertain glance at her—and then went back to hauling off his theatre gear.

'When I came here I stipulated to the hospital board that they keep the theatre well equipped. I have an anaesthetist come down from Boquadale once a week. Since I've been here we've been able to do a lot of surgery. It saves the locals the long trip to Brisbane and it keeps my hand in.' His voice was clipped, efficient, moving on.

'So you'll be able to go back to the States and move on from where you left off,' she whispered. 'You're a fine surgeon, Dev.'

'You're not so bad as an anaesthetist yourself.'

'If I stay here—if you leave—then I won't be able to do surgery. I'm no surgeon.'

'No.' He hesitated. 'But the locals have used Brisbane before.'

'But today...Katy would have died if there'd been only one doctor here.'

'You do the best you can,' he said, almost roughly. 'You can't beat yourself up when it doesn't work. I've learned that, living here. I'm not two doctors and I can't feel guilty because I can't do two jobs.'

He'd shed all his theatre gear now, and was back in his casual trousers and open-necked shirt. He glanced at her—still uncertain—and then crossed to the sink and started to wash.

'But you... You definitely want to stay?'

'I want to stay.'

'Why?'

'This is my home.' Her whisper faltered. She clenched her fingers into her palms and they hurt, but she made herself go on. He was being efficient, clinical, moving on. She had to make him see.

'Dev, I've never felt like this.'

'Don't!' It was a harsh exclamation and it made her gaze jerk upward.

'What?'

'You and me...'

'I didn't mean that,' she told him. He sounded angry, but all of a sudden she was angry, too. 'Oh, it's there. I know you don't want it and I accept that it's a crazy imposition, me throwing myself at you like this. Your brother's widow falling in love with you and telling you so, like a crazy, lovesick teenager. It's stupid. I accept that it's stupid. The only reason I've done it is that after so many deaths—my parents and my time in Ethiopia and then Corey—it's taught me that when you feel something you say it. If you wait until tomorrow, then tomorrow might never arrive.'

'I don't want—'

'I know you don't want,' she said wearily, putting a hand to her eyes and letting herself indulge in a moment's darkness. 'And I'm pushing it no further. You needn't fear, Dev. I have no intention of following behind you for the rest of your life. Or even saying...what I've already said, ever again. I won't. But I am staying here.' She glanced

up at him again, trying for defiance. 'Not necessarily in your house,' she told him, 'though Lorna
wants me to. Certainly not in your house if you
decide to stay on as well. I'll buy myself a place
in town. But, regardless of what you do, I want to
stay here. I want to bring up Corey's child here.'

'Regardless of what I do?' He was staring at her
like he'd have stared at a loaded gun. 'So I have
no say in it?'

'You have no say in what I do. No.'

'I'm the doctor here. If I don't want you—'

'Dev, there're three alternatives,' she interrupted. 'As I told you, I'm independent. I don't
need to ask favours. I can decide. If you stay here
and you want to work as you have before, alone,
then I'll stay out of your way as much as I can.
Maybe I'll set up a small private practice that's not
dependent on your goodwill. Alternatively, if you
can bear to work along side me and you decide to
stay, you can offer me a job as your partner. Or
you can do as I believe you wish and go back to
the States.'

He was gazing at her as if she'd suddenly
sprung two heads. 'But I still have no say…'

'In whether I stay or not? No.' She rose wearily
to her feet, putting her hand to her aching back.
Her baby was suddenly unbearably heavy. 'Let's
leave it,' she said wearily. 'I need to get back to
my party.'

'Your party?'

'Don't be dumb,' she snapped. 'My working bee. The one where the entire community is doing something for you as well as for Corey and Kyle. The working bee you refused to attend.'

'You think I'm being petty.'

'Of course you're being petty. They're working on your garden.'

He closed his eyes. Maybe he needed time out, too, she thought. Maybe.

But she couldn't afford to be sympathetic. She had so many things going in her own head that if she tried to empathise with Dev she felt like she'd fall over.

'It doesn't feel like my garden,' he said, and she snapped again.

'Because you've blocked it off. It was part of Corey, part of the family you thought you let down. Get over it, Dev.'

'Do we have to do the psychoanalysis bit?'

'I guess we don't,' she told him, sighing. 'OK. Enough. You go off and do what you have to do. I need to find my gumboots and find some way of getting back to the house.'

'Your gumboots are at the entrance,' he told her, and even managed a smile. 'Not that I object to your socks.'

That caught her. She glanced down.

She'd forgotten she was wearing these socks.

The gumboots she'd been wearing had been Lorna's and they were two sizes too big. So this morning, trying to figure out some way she could wear the big rubber boots that served her well when working in the undergrowth, she'd searched the house for thick socks. She'd found football gear. The socks were huge and thick and they made her feet fit the boots beautifully. They were great.

They had bright red and yellow stripes, and black toes.

'Karington football club,' Dev said faintly. 'I know you think that you belong, but isn't this is taking things to extremes?'

'I'll do whatever I must to belong,' she said— with dignity.

He choked. That gorgeous smile appeared again. It had been gone for too long, she thought. 'I know you will.'

'Dev…'

'Em.' He moved aside a little so she could pass. So she could march out into the corridor and leave, her dignity intact, with her glorious red maternity tent and her glorious socks.

She tilted her chin and marched.

'Em.'

She'd reached him. She was right by him. Her arm was brushing his.

She glanced sideways up at him.

Mistake.

The smile had faded.

He was looking down at her with such an expression...

Such an expression...

She stopped. Of course she stopped. When a man was looking at a woman as Dev was looking at her...

'Dev...'

'I can't,' he told her, and she felt her heart twist inside her. His words held a pain that was well nigh unbearable.

'I'm just a woman, Dev,' she said softly. 'What's the problem?'

'Hell, Em, you don't make it easy.'

'No.'

She didn't move. She should. Walk, she told her feet, but there was something happening here that was more powerful than any message she could give her stupid, football-sock-clad toes.

'Do you want me to kiss you?' he asked, and she almost laughed. Almost.

'Do you want to? A crazy red tent with stripy socks? Why would you want to kiss me, Dev?'

'Why indeed?'

'So don't,' she whispered, and somehow she made her toes take a step away.

He stopped her. His hands came to rest on her shoulders. She paused and he twisted her around so they were facing each other.

Almost facing each other. Not quite. Her nose came just to his chin. She concentrated on the pulse in his neck, beating, beating.

'Em, I can't.'

'So don't.'

'I can't.' But it was never going to be the truth.

Because, of course, he could. His hand was under her chin, tilting her face upward so that her eyes met his. So that the link that she'd felt the moment she'd seen this man slammed back a thousandfold.

He was smiling down at her. Smiling. His eyes were questioning. They were quizzical, puzzled, but still they were smiling.

'I think… I need to kiss you anyway,' he murmured.

'Because of the socks?' she managed. 'Irresistible, huh?'

'Irresistible,' he agreed.

But then there was room for nothing else. Not for laughter. Not for smiles. Not for reflections on her crazy, sexless attire. His mouth was lowering on hers—and her world shut down right then.

How could she have thought this man was like Corey? How could she have thought he was like anyone?

He was Dev.

His lips touched hers and her senses shuttered down, slammed closed, leaving room for nothing, no one but Dev.

Devlin O'Halloran.

Her home.

He had no intention of kissing her.

Of course he hadn't. Why should he? She was nothing to do with him. Somehow he had to get to know this woman as his brother's widow.

But not fall in love with her.

He wasn't falling in love, he told himself desperately. He wasn't. So he shouldn't kiss her.

But she'd walked past him, she'd brushed his body, she smelt of new-mown grass, and rosewater and soap and antiseptic and…and…

She smelled of Emma.

Her hair was as mass of crazy curls, tendrils escaping every which way from the knot she'd tied it into this morning. There was a tendril wisping into her eyes right now.

And her eyes. Deep green. Luminescent. Questioning. Trusting.

Loving?

She'd said she'd fallen in love with him, he thought, dazed. How could she have?

He loved Margaret—didn't he? He loved a cool, svelte, beautiful woman who kept her emotions tightly under control. He didn't love this pregnant, crazy, football-socked eruption of chaos.

But she was right beside him. Her eyes were on his. There was this charge between them. This feeling he didn't understand, this force he couldn't fight.

So he kissed her. Of course he kissed her.

It was as if there were two of him—the sensible Dev O'Halloran who in a few weeks would pack up here and move back to the States, back to his sensible, logical life, saying thank you gratefully to Emma and maybe taking the lovely Margaret with him. As his wife.

And then there was the Dev who was here now. The Dev who overpoweringly told the sensible Dev to take himself off and not watch what the crazy Dev was doing. The Dev who was tilting Emma's lips to his. Whose mouth was lowering…

She was just lovely. She was the most desirable thing.

Emma.

Their mouths met, locked, merged. His arms were around her, holding her close, closer…

Her breasts were moulding themselves to him, each curve fitting into place as if she belonged right there. It was as if they'd been like some crazy, mixed-up puzzle of a jigsaw—a puzzle that had been once been his life—and suddenly the pieces of the puzzle were sliding into place.

Sliding home.

The sensation was unbelievably sweet. Unbelievably wonderful.

Unbelievably right.

His mouth was searching, deepening the kiss, aching to explore this sensation that was as unexpected as it was amazing. She tasted of her own sweet self, he thought, a confusing changeling, an unknown, a woman he'd never thought he could desire.

Up until this moment Dev would have been able to describe the woman of his dreams. Tall. Cool. Beautiful. Career-based. Intelligent and self-assured.

Not squat, curly, bossy, pregnant…

Not Em.

It didn't matter. How could it matter? Or maybe it did—maybe the sensible Dev would somehow step in again in the future—but how could he think of that now? But it surely didn't matter now. How could he think of anything but the taste of her, the feel of her, the wanting…

She was sinking into him and he was gathering her tight against him. He heard a tiny whimper of pleasure as her hands twisted around his head, her fingers raked his hair, pulling him closer, deepening the kiss.

Deepening the love.

Em.

Something kicked him.

The sensation was unbelievable. It was so astonishing that he drew away, just a little. Confused, he stared down into Emma's eyes and there was laughter there. Laughter!

'I think we're being censored,' she told him, her voice husky with a passion that matched the dazed pleasure behind her eyes. 'Do you mind? We can hardly move to another room.'

'The baby…'

She smiled, but her smile was suddenly a trace uncertain. Her eyes said she knew and regretted—infinitely regretted—that the moment had been broken, for she might not get it back. 'He'd better get used to his mother kissing the guy she loves,' she whispered.

That silenced him. It floored him. The whole damn situation floored him. He was still holding her, but instead of pulling her back into him, continuing the kiss, he held her slightly back. Rigid. Putting a barrier between them.

Hell, it hurt, but did he have a choice?

The sensible Dev had to have room here.

'You love me?'

'You know that I do, Dev,' she said evenly. 'I'm sorry.' Her eyes were searching his, honest, open, trusting. 'I know you don't want it. Or you don't think you want it. But I can't help it, you know. I just…do.'

She faltered. She was trying to be pragmatic but she wasn't succeeding. 'What about you?'

'I can't…' He shook his head. 'Em, this relationship is crazy. Love? So fast? It isn't possible. And even if it was, how do you think it'd make me feel about Corey?'

'More guilt? You think that's logical? Corey would love this.'

'It's not the least bit logical,' he snapped. Hell, if only she wouldn't keep looking at him. She was driving him crazy, just being here. 'Nothing's logical. But if you think I can stay here calmly and take over Corey's life…'

'Is that what you think I'm asking you to do?'

'I don't know what you're asking.'

'I'm not asking anything.' Her voice steadied then, and her eyes became calmly watchful. 'No one's asking anything of you, Dev. On the contrary, you're being offered what you most want. A way out of this town. All you have to do is put me away, tell me I'm being ridiculous with this love business, say goodbye to your mother and leave. With or without Margaret. That's what I'm offering. But I am also offering alternatives. You need to see them. You need to know what they are. Anything less than the truth will only lead to heartache.'

'More heartache.'

Deep breath. She eyed him with caution—and then with anger. Rising anger. 'You think it's easy telling you I love you?' she demanded. 'You great twit, get a bit of sensitivity here.' But it seemed she was too weary to sustain anger. Too...defeated? She sighed and turned away, hauling open the door. 'Enough. I'm going back to the house.'

'Margaret and I will take you.' Somehow he made his voice work. Somehow he managed to be practical 'We...we planned to go out there for a bit.'

'Good of you,' she said wryly. 'But there is an excuse if you need one. After all, someone needs to stay with Katy.'

'Don't tell me how to run my medical practice,' he snapped. 'You're telling me how to run everything else.'

'I'm not telling you.' She sounded hurt. 'I'm offering.'

'Butt out, Emma.'

'Yes, sir.'

Drat the woman. Just when he thought he had her pegged she turned into something else. A chameleon. Beloved chameleon. No, not beloved. Not. She couldn't be. 'I'll check on Katy and then we'll go,' he told her. 'I'll only stay out there for a few minutes.'

'So Katy will be your excuse to leave.'

'Don't do this to me.'

'No, sir.' Damn, she was smiling. There was laughter behind her eyes. He ought to...

Kiss her again?

No.

'Ten minutes out the front,' he told her, and she had the effrontery to snap her heels together, raise her hand in salute and grin.

'Yes, sir.'

'Emma...'

'Yes, sir?'

'Butt out of my life.'

'Maybe.'

She was dumb.

Why on earth had she showed him her heart? She was dumb, dumb, dumb.

'He has a right to know.

'He's going to be your baby's uncle. How the heck can you stay friendly with him after this?

'How can I stay friendly anyway?

'He thinks I'm stupid.

'You are stupid.'

The baby kicked again and she glared down at her bump. 'And you, what do you think you're doing, kicking the man I love? You dumb baby, don't know you this is important?'

It wasn't important. It was...nothing.

She stared down at her bump for a while longer. Her baby was squirming, alive and growing beneath her heart.

'It's me who's dumb,' she told her baby. 'There's just you and me, sweetheart. We know that. We've always known that. I'm just sighing for the moon.'

No. Sighing for Dev.

CHAPTER TEN

THE journey back out to the house was made in almost complete silence. Dev drove. Margaret sat in the front passenger seat. Neither talked, though occasionally Margaret glanced sideways uncertainly at Dev, as though sensing there was something going on that she wasn't privy to.

Meanwhile Emma sat in the back and tried not to think uncharitable thoughts about beautifully matched couples who charitably gave poor single mothers a drive home.

'Lorna tells me you may stay in Karington,' Margaret said at one stage—brightly—and Emma tried for a bright reply.

'Yep. I fancy having a grandma for my baby, and Lorna loves the idea.'

'That'd be wonderful,' Margaret said serenely. 'For us, too. It'll free Dev up to decide what he wants to do. If Dev decides to stay here, or if we come back for visits later on...'

'Then our children might end up being friends,' Emma said, seeing where the conversation was headed and getting in early. 'After all, they'll be cousins. I'll probably stop at one, but how many do you two intend having?'

There was a sound between a choke and a cough from the driver's seat and both women looked at Dev with varying degrees of concern.

And both women decided that silence might be the best way to go.

At least the ride was short. The tension would disappear once everyone was around, Emma thought thankfully, and when they arrived she was relieved to find that there were cars still surrounding the house. The barbecue lunch would be long finished. It was time for the working bee to end— but obviously no one had felt like leaving.

Kyle's dad had stayed for the entire operation, hovering with Katy's parents, desperate that another death would not be added to his tragedy, and he must have brought the news back to the house. Katy would live—and as soon as Dev's car drew up, a resounding cheer erupted from every person present.

The applause went on and on. Conquering sports heroes couldn't have received a more joyous reception. This was a far call from her impersonal city medicine back in London, Emma thought, stunned.

'Get used to it, Em,' she heard Dev say, and she managed a smile.

'It's wonderful. It's fantastic that we saved Katy and it's magic that the whole community shares our delight. Don't you think it's amazing?'

He cast her a curious glance. 'You like the praise?'

'No.' She flushed. 'That's a mean thing to say, Dev O'Halloran, and you know it. Of course it's not the praise. You think that's why I'm happy?'

His gaze rested on her face for a long moment and finally he gave a rueful smile. 'You get me every time.'

'What do you mean?'

'I'm sorry. That was unfair. You're right in that I was being mean. You surely deserve any applause you get.'

'It's not that I deserve it,' she said, struggling to make him see. 'I like…just knowing everyone. Just being part of this. To leave of your own free will…' She shook her head in disbelief that he could contemplate such a thing.

But their conversation couldn't continue. She was being distracted from all sides. People had been waiting for her to arrive, and their impatience couldn't be held in check.

'Hey, Dr Em, we have a surprise for you,' someone called.

'You haven't painted my bedroom purple?' she called back in mock horror, and there was general laughter.

'Nope,' the voice called. 'Better'n a bedroom. How about someone to share it with?' Once more there was laughter. The crowd parted—and out stepped Paul.

Paul.

She'd had enough shocks for one day. She stood, rooted to the spot, staring at the man she'd once agreed to marry.

Paul.

He was lovely. She looked at him as he strode through the crowd with his hands held out to greet her. He was tall and blond and open-faced, with a wide, white smile and almost boyish good looks. He was close to forty but he looked about twenty-five. He was the best orthopaedic surgeon she knew.

He was her best friend.

'Paul.'

Then he was with her, taking her hands, holding her away from him, smiling into her stunned face—and then sweeping her into his arms and solidly kissing her while the crowd around them erupted into even more applause.

She let him kiss her. How could she not? To struggle away, with such an audience, was impossible.

So he kissed her and she felt pleasure that her friend was here.

She felt concern and guilt and distress that he'd come so far for nothing.

She felt not a trace of the surge of joy she'd felt as Dev had held her.

Finally he released her and held her again at arm's length, still smiling. Had he not noticed there was nothing between them? she wondered. Maybe he didn't know what that something could be.

Maybe he'd never met his link. His other half. The person who was right.

'Dear Em.' He was smiling at her with real affection as he glanced down at her bulge. 'You've got fatter.'

'Thank you very much,' she managed. 'Paul, what are you doing here?'

He hesitated. Their audience was dispersing now—a little—giving them space. Dev and Margaret were still there, though. Not three yards away. Listening to every word, Emma thought grimly. Yeah, Dev would really like this.

Paul was speaking. She had to listen.

'I knew you wouldn't really mean it,' he told her. 'Breaking off our engagement like this is crazy. It's all your ridiculous scruples. I was so worried, Em dear, and when you said you'd been in an accident I worried even more. So I rang Devlin.'

'Devlin?'

'I rang the hospital and asked who was in charge. Devlin talked to me. He said you were confused and upset and unsure as to your future.'

'Confused and upset.' She turned to face Dev. 'Yeah? Is that what you said?'

'I asked Devlin if he thought I should come and he agreed.' Paul turned and smiled at Dev, holding out his hand in greeting. 'So you're Devlin.'

'He's Dr O'Halloran,' Emma said meaningfully. 'Same as me. Unsure as to my future, is he?'

'And this is?' Paul's eyes had moved on—appreciatively—to Margaret.

'This is Devlin's fiancée,' Emma told him. 'She's sure about her future.'

'Hey,' Dev said.

'Confused and upset, eh?' Emma said—and glowered.

'You were upset,' Dev said, and there wasn't the faintest trace of apology in his voice. 'I thought Paul should come and talk some sense into you.'

'Like you need Margaret to talk some sense into you,' she retorted, thoroughly ruffled. 'Re marriage.'

'Dev doesn't need sense talked into him,' Margaret offered, and then paused. 'He's already sensible. I mean, we want… At least I think we want…'

'You sound as confused as I am,' Paul told her, sensing a kindred spirit. 'For heaven's sake, Em, how hard is it to say you'll marry me?'

'Devlin's like that,' Margaret told him. 'I mean, we've known each other for ever and it's the only sensible thing to do.'

'But will they see it?' Paul demanded, and raked his hand through his boyish fair hair in shared exasperation. 'Hell.'

'My mother so wants a white wedding,' Margaret told him. 'I have three sisters who want to be bridesmaids.'

'Me, too,' Paul told her. 'But, of course, with Em in this condition…'

'You mean fat?' Emma said dangerously.

They weren't listening. 'Yeah, a white wedding would be impossible,' Margaret agreed. 'You'll have to wait until after the baby's born and even then, white's hardly appropriate. But Dev just wants a registry office.'

'I did not say registry office,' Dev managed.

'You did. Last year when I said if we did get married how many bridesmaids would you like?'

'That was hypothetical.'

'You see what I'm up against?' Margaret demanded of Paul.

'Indecisive partners,' Paul agreed.

'Decisive partners,' Emma snapped. 'We're not marrying anyone.'

'Hey, she's not speaking for Dev,' Margaret said, startled. 'Is she, Dev?'

'No, I...' Dev floundered.

'Why aren't you marrying me?' Paul asked Emma.

'Because I hate soccer,' Emma said, desperately searching for something that could possibly make sense to the man.

'You hate soccer?' Margaret stared at her as if she'd just landed from outer space. 'How can you possibly hate soccer? When Australia is almost guaranteed a place in the next World Cup?'

'Now, that's not right,' Paul said, and Margaret looked at him as if he'd uttered blasphemy.

'How can you say that? We've worked so hard. How many of our Australian players are over there, playing their hearts out for English or European sides, when they should have the motivation to play here?'

'You have had some great players,' Paul conceded. 'Harry Kewell...'

'Oh, isn't he the best?' Margaret breathed. 'Goal try for Australia when we beat England—'

'I was there.'

'You were there!'

'Excuse me,' Emma said. She was wavering toward the hysterical here. Hysteria seemed a very good option.

'Maybe you'd better go and check your purple bedroom,' Dev told her, grinning. 'While our assorted partners sort out the rights and wrongs of world soccer.'

'Paul's not my—'

She was cut off in mid-sentence.

From out on the road, from the bend just before the driveway meandered towards Dev's house, there was the sound of a crash.

An almighty crash. Metal. Splintering wood. A scream, cut short.

The crash went on and on, reverberating in the stillness of the tropical afternoon.

'The cliff.' It was Dev. 'Oh, God, the road. The bend…'

'Someone's gone over.' It was a man's shout from up on the veranda where he could see glimpses through the trees. 'Hell. A truck.'

No more drama. There was part of Emma that just wanted to shut down right then. That had had enough.

'What…?'

'The road surface was damaged when the bus went over,' Dev snapped. He was already running, heading to his car. 'The side of the road gave a bit when the bus went over and the tow-truck made it worse. I rang the council and said there should be rails. Of all the stupid…'

'I'll come.' She was already moving.

But Dev stopped her. 'No.' Dev was decisive. 'Em, you've done enough today. You'll risk the baby. Stay.' He was behind the wheel and Margaret was piling in beside him.

'Hey, I'm a doctor, too,' Paul yelled, and dived in after them.

Margaret even smiled.

The car gunned off down the drive and Emma was left staring.

Dev, carrying medical supplies, was the only one who drove the few hundred yards to where the truck had crashed. The other men of the party ran or walked with varying degrees of trepidation.

Women and children held back.

It had been a very loud crash, a horrific crash, and maybe it was someone they knew, and staying behind when the men were involved was pretty darn hard.

Dear God, not more death...

Emma forced her feet to stay where they were.

'Stay,' she told herself. 'There're two doctors and a nurse there already. Stay.'

'We'd just get in the way,' Lorna said—uncertainly—and Emma agreed.

Sort of.

Around her the women were saying the same thing to the kids. 'We'd just get in the way.' But they were looking at each other, uncertain. Fearful. Eyes reflecting horror.

Surely imagined horror had to be worse than reality. Surely...

No one moved.

'I can't bear it,' one of the mothers said, and burst into tears.

Nothing.

'Maybe if a truck's over the edge like the bus, they'll need everyone to stop it slipping till the crane arrives.' It was Robbie Sims, tremulous. Fearful.

They all thought about it. There'd been four or five men who'd taken off down the track but...

'None of them took rope,' Mrs Sims said.

'We've got a rope in the shed,' Lorna told them—and a decision was made. Anything was better than not knowing.

'OK, Robbie, you grab the rope,' his mother told him. 'You can come—in case you need to help—carry that, but stay with us and don't run on ahead.'

And Jemima's mother said, 'Maybe they'll need everyone. Jemima, hold my hand.'

And they all headed out along the drive to see.

Not Emma. Dev had said stay.

Not Lorna. She was being a loyal mother-in-law.

'We could just go to the end of the drive and...and look,' Lorna said. 'I mean, you have your cellphone, dear. You could relay messages.'

Of course. Excellent idea, Emma decided. She was going nuts.

'It sounded awful,' she said as they walked.

'It can't be awful,' Lorna whispered. 'It just can't be. But we need to see.'

'Yes.'

So Emma walked down the drive, Lorna beside her, fussing, worrying that she'd done too much and that the excitement might be bad for the baby.

'This baby's used to excitement,' Emma told her. 'By the way, you do realise that you'll make an excellent grandma.'

Lorna gave her a distracted smile. 'I do hope so. But now... Do you think this is serious? Oh, my dear...'

'It sounded serious.' Emma grimaced. 'But I hope it's not. I'm sick of serious.'

'Oh, my dear, me, too,' Lorna said, and hesitated. They'd come this far and suddenly there was a part of both of them that didn't want to go further. 'Do you think...maybe we ought to go back to the house. Boil water or something?'

'I don't think I'm a stay at the house and boil water sort of person,' Emma said cautiously, and Lorna even managed a smile.

'Me neither. But we can hope...'

And then they rounded the bend—and saw.

*   *   *

As calamities went, it was a calamity—but maybe not on the scale of the school bus.

A truck had veered off the road, slipping on the crumpling road verge. The driver had panicked and overcorrected, slamming into the cliff on the safe side of the road.

The truck had been loaded with crates. The crates were now spread over the road. Some of the crates had smashed.

The cargo was everywhere.

Emma stared, unable to believe her eyes.

'It's ducklings,' Lorna breathed.

Ducklings.

There were indeed ducklings. Tiny blobs of yellow scattering in all directions.

And then they met their first duck.

Jemima had already caught one. She'd been in the leading pack of mums and kids, and now the little girl came running back up the track, pop-eyed with excitement.

'There're ducklings everywhere,' she breathed. 'Dad said I had to get a box to put them in. Dr O'Halloran said there's boxes under the stairs.'

'Ducklings,' Emma said cautiously, unable to believe her eyes.

'Yeah, look.' Jemima opened her hand. A tiny yellow ball of fluff was cradled in her palm. 'There were crates of ducklings on the back of the truck and the truck hit the cliff and the crates fell off and there're ducklings everywhere.'

'Goodness,' Lorna said faintly, glancing ahead with worry. Moving on to fear. 'Is anyone hurt?'

'Only a lady with a sore arm,' Jemima said. 'There's hardly even any blood—and no one's dead.'

'G-good,' Emma managed, and looked again at the scattering blobs. 'How many ducklings?'

'Millions and millions.'

There weren't millions and millions—but there were a lot.

'Well!' As they took on board the sight of the crashed truck and the ducklings, Lorna moved into exasperation mode. 'I might have known. Ruby Hyde.'

'You know her?' Emma was still trying to take it all in. There were kids darting everywhere, chasing fluffballs.

Where was Dev?

Around the other side of the crashed truck?

'Ruby runs a wildlife shelter of sorts just north of the park,' Lorna told her. 'She has a huge lake on her land, and she has a licence to sell duck eggs. But she's the most disorganised businesswoman I know. Not only do her ducks lay only very occasionally anywhere where Ruby can find the eggs to collect them, she can't even organise them to produce babies. So every year she buys ducklings.

These ducklings will have it made—if they finally make it to Ruby's. This lot will lounge around on the lake, they'll never be culled for dinner or because they're not laying, they'll die of old age after being fed by Lady Bountiful for years and years... Ruby's ducks are legend.' Lorna grimaced in disapproval as she looked at the chaos in front of her and then she relented. 'I do hope she's all right. She might be a hopeless businesswoman but we're all fond of her. Very fond.'

So what was happening? They moved closer, around the truck.

Farce gave way to concern. Ruby didn't look all right, Emma thought, starting to worry about a lady she'd never met but felt an intuitive sympathy for. Ruby, owner of duck paradise. The middle-aged lady was lying on the ground, unmoving, and Dev and Paul and Margaret were working over her. Emma could see a drip being set up.

'I'll check,' she told Lorna, moving closer
'Watch out for ducklings.'

But the ducklings were being taken care of. Emma's working bee—twenty kids or so—had now been diverted into a duck collection squad.

'They're so cute.' It was Chrissy Martin of 'she wants to be a doctor' fame, staring down at a fluffball in each hand. 'Do you think we'd be allowed to keep one?'

'One's done something on my fingers.' It was Robbie. 'Yuck.' He opened his palm and eyed his charge with caution. And then grinned. These kids had come here fearing more tragedy and instead had found ducks. 'They are kinda cute. How long do you reckon it'll take Jemima to bring back those boxes? Ooh, there's another. I've run out of hands.'

'Let me help, dear.' Lorna was already on her hands and knees, reaching for a duckling who was headed for the cliff and the sea and freedom. Of a sort. 'No, dear, you don't want to go there. There're sharks in the sea, and sharks eat ducks.'

Yep, she'd make a great grandma, Emma thought with appreciation. But she was focussed now on Ruby. She made her way carefully towards the medical tableau, careful of feet and darting ducklings.

What she saw made her fear recede. It was bad—but it wasn't dreadful.

Ruby was conscious. She appeared to be breathing normally. As Jem had said, there was little blood. Dev wasn't using oxygen, though Emma knew he had it if needed. That was a good sign.

'What do you think you're doing?'

It was Dev, glancing up and letting his face darken with displeasure as he saw who was behind him. 'I thought I told you to stay put.'

'I wondered whether you'd need a paediatrician,' she told him, meeting his eyes with a look that wasn't even defiant. She'd gone past that with this man. 'And I was right.' She glanced around her at assorted ducklings. 'Many of these children are far too young to leave their mothers. What problems are you having with *your* patient?'

His face relaxed a little. A little. If he smiled he'd crack his face, Emma thought. Did he have to be so crabby?

'Nothing that we need you for,' he told her, and she almost glowered.

'Gee, thanks very much.' But it wasn't the time for continuing what was between them. Her eyes were on Ruby, assessing. What she saw reassured her even more. There was seemingly no facial or head damage and little bleeding, apart from what looked like superficial scratches. Ruby's face was starting to relax, and Emma guessed that morphine had been administered and was already taking effect.

'What's happening?' she asked, softly, and Dev moved back into doctor mode. A mode they could both handle.

'It looks as if she's shattered her collar-bone,' Dev told her, watching her assessment and knowing she was seeing what he'd already seen. Deciding it was useless to block her out completely. 'But that seems to be the extent of the damage. We'll take her straight to Theatre. Paul's offered to set it for us.'

Of course. Paul was an excellent orthopaedic surgeon.

'How fortunate that Paul's here,' Emma said faintly, and Margaret looked up and smiled. Brightly. At Paul.

'Isn't it? We're so lucky.'

'I don't feel lucky,' Ruby muttered from under their ministering hands, and Emma smiled in turn, but down at Ruby, and it was designed as a comfort smile.

'I guess you don't,' she told her. 'But my friend Paul is the best orthopaedic surgeon I know and you'll be in the best of hands.'

'I'll help,' Margaret said—and then she coloured as if she suddenly realised she was sounding goofy.

Goodness, Emma thought. Goodness. She stared at Margaret—and then she stared at Paul.

They were two matching shades of blush-pink.

Goodness!

Who didn't believe in love at first sight?

'You don't need me?' she asked, trying not to smile.

'No, Em,' Dev said gently. 'We don't need you. Go home and put your feet up.'

'Yeah, right.'

'Honest, Em,' he told her. 'We'll manage just fine without you.'

Them managing fine was all very well, Emma thought crossly. It was fine not to be needed when you didn't want to be needed. But she wanted to be needed.

With the ducklings dispersed to every household in Karington, with the mess from the day's work cleared up by the various mums and dads before they went, with the house as organised, painted and clean as it had ever been in anyone's living memory, there was certainly time to put her feet up.

She was alone.

Lorna had offered to stay but she was duck-sitting two ducklings herself and had decided she had a heat bag at home and maybe they'd be better settled where they'd stay the night. She clucked over Emma a little—but the ducklings were clearly distracting, and finally she left to duck-sit in earnest.

The house was deserted.

So now what?

Put your feet up, Emma told herself.

She couldn't. It seemed almost physically impossible.

Dev and Paul and Margaret were operating at this minute. They were working without her.

She wanted to be there.

'It's not fair,' she told her bump. 'If it wasn't for you I'd be in there up to my elbows.

'They didn't want you. They wouldn't want you even if you weren't pregnant. No one wants you.

'So what's new?

'Ooh, why don't you find a whisky bottle and sing the blues? For heaven's sake, woman, get a grip. You're used to alone.'

Which was just the problem. She was accustomed to being alone and she knew how hard it was. She had to get used to being more alone.

'No. I'll have this community.

'It's not just this community you want.

'No. But Dev's going back to America. He doesn't need you. Like he doesn't need you now.'

What to do? What?

Disconsolate and inclined to be huffy, she took herself down to the beach to sulk.

Which achieved nothing.

The beach was as near to perfection as it was possible for a beach to be. The moon was rising over the horizon, a sliver of gold sending shards of light glimmering over the waves.

'Don't do your romantic thing to me,' she muttered. 'What earthly use is a beach and moonlight without…?

'Without what?

'Without who?'

She was achy. Her legs were cramping a bit. She'd sat too long in one position during the operation this morning and she was paying the price.

'So take a walk,' she told herself.

'Along a moonlit beach. Yeah, right.'

She glowered at the moon and turned her face away from it. She'd walk back along the road, she told herself. Just up to the first bend and back again. Past the place where everything kept crashing. One of the men had told her they were putting barricades and lamps along the verge. Had it been done yet?

She could look.

So she trudged along the road and tried not to think uncharitable thoughts about people who were doing really interesting medicine without her and people who were discriminating against her just because she was pregnant and wouldn't let her help and wouldn't let her near and...

And she wasn't being very sensible.

She reached the place where the bus had rolled. Where the truck had crashed. There'd been so many ducklings. Sixty or seventy, she thought.

Maybe someone should have asked Ruby how many there were.

Yeah, let's set up a duckling roll-call, she told herself, chiding herself for being ridiculous. But even so...

The moon was playing on the cliff. There was a temporary barrier on the verge. She leant over and gazed down the cliff face.

There was a crate, washing in and out on the waves.

She stared.

It was a wooden crate. The same as the ones the ducklings had been in.

Why hadn't it sunk?

She thought back to the one intact crate she'd seen that afternoon. The bottom and top had been solid wood, with solid wooden slats coming about two inches up the side. There were slits along the side to let in air.

The shape it was, it'd act as a boat.

It was a still night. No wind. The waves were slopping against the cliff.

The crate was being thumped against the rocks.

It didn't look smashed, she thought in increasing dismay. That meant…that meant it was probably still full of ducklings.

She needed the lifeguard, she thought. What chance of the lifeguard coming out to rescue a few ducks?

But then a wave, bigger than most, pushed the crate further in, shoving it firmly between two rocks. The crate wedged in hard and stuck.

Emma watched in growing distress as a few more waves hit it.

Each wave washed through the crate. The crate didn't float free.

The tide was coming in.

'They're probably already dead,' she told herself, horrified. 'They're probably...'

Another wave washed in, and out again. The crate was being completely filled with water and then emptied.

The tide was coming in. Soon it wouldn't empty.

'They're only ducks.

'Yeah, and I'm only human. I can't bear this.'

She stared at the cliff, assessing. It wasn't so steep. Was it?

No. It wasn't too steep. If she was careful she could get down there and dislodge the crate. She might not be able to get the crate up the cliff again but she could wedge it higher than the high-tide mark and then go and get help.

For some dead ducks?

'They're not dead,' she said it out loud. For some reason it was absurdly important, and she repeated it just to make sure. 'They're not dead.'

OK. Do it, girl.

So, cautiously—very cautiously, for she was no fool—she climbed over the barricade.

'I used to be great at climbing trees.

'This is a cliff and you're seven months pregnant.

'Piece of cake. You can do it.

'You're actually seven and a half months.

'So this kid's gotta learn to climb. Go, girl.'

Right.

She got herself six feet down. Ten feet down.

It was pretty far down.

Fifteen feet.

Damned ducks.

Eighteen.

The rock she'd just stepped on dislodged and dropped into the sea.

Whoops.

She managed to get lower but looked ruefully at the place where the rock had been.

That had been her foothold. How was she to get up again?

Worry about that afterwards.

After?

After you've rescued your ducks.

Another step.

Another.

She found herself a secure toehold, reached down and hauled the crate up. She heard faint cheeps.

Hey, they were alive. Alive!

'You guys might be mending collar-bones,' she told her absent medical colleagues. 'But I'm saving ducks!'

They were heavy. Really heavy. She thought of breaking open a side and letting them climb up themselves but then... How did you tell a duckling to climb? Would a duckling know that up meant safety?

She thought of Lorna's advice to her ducklings a couple of hours ago.

'No, dear, you don't want to go there. There're sharks in the sea, and sharks eat ducks.'

Right. Pick the damned crate up and get it above the high-tide mark.

And somehow she did. Somewhere she'd read that people could do extraordinary things under pressure—lift twenty-ton trucks when their kid was underneath. Maybe this wasn't the same thing but by the time her crate had been shoved onto a ledge that was dry and secure, she felt like she'd done just that.

They were safe. The crate was cheeping. She'd done it.

'You guys owe me an omelette a day for life,' she told them. 'Put it in your diary.'

Now all she had to do was get up again.

She couldn't.

She clambered three feet up. The rock she'd used for a foothold wasn't there.

There was nothing else to support her.

Whoops.

She returned to base. Her ducklings were still cheeping.

'Any ideas?'

Nope.

Oh, heck, she was stuck. Dismay washed over her like a grey fog. There weren't any ideas.

She was going to have to wait and be rescued.

Somebody would rescue her, she told herself, feeling desperate. Come dawn, maybe the local fishermen would see her from the sea.

Come dawn?

Aargh!

'Let's not get hysterical here. Stay calm. It's not like you're alone. You have ducklings.

'You guys mind some company?'

Cheep.

'Right, then.' She sighed and shoved the crate as far along the ledge as she could manage. That left her room to sit. Not exactly comfortably.

'When will they miss me?' she asked the ducks.

That was a scary thought. Dev wouldn't come home. Tomorrow was Monday but there had been a general consensus that work on the house be put on hold for tomorrow. Every kid was duck-sitting.

'Which means no one will come to the house.

'Someone will come,' she told the ducks. 'If the fishermen don't see me then Lorna will come.

'Lorna has her own ducklings to take care of.

'Paul will come.

'Are you kidding? Did you see the way he looked at Margaret?

'He came all the way from England to see you.

'So he might…

'He might not.'

That wasn't a good thought. She sniffed.

'If I cry,' she told herself, 'I'm just plain going to wail here. I'm pathetic. Pathetic, pathetic, pathetic.'

She sniffed again.

'Are you guys cold?' she asked the ducklings. 'Hungry? Thirsty? And tired? You are? Well, that makes ten of us. Or twenty. How many of you are in there?'

'Cheep.'

'I'll try to sleep, counting ducklings,' she told them.

She wriggled further onto her ledge, encountering the odd bump of very hard rock and acknowledged that sleep was an impossibility.

'OK, I'm nuts. I won't sleep. I'll just sit here and think dark thoughts about men and life and ducklings. And I'll try very hard not to think about roast duck.'

CHAPTER ELEVEN

WITH Ruby's collar-bone successfully pinned—Dev was relieved to find that Paul really was an excellent orthopaedic surgeon—Margaret offered to take Paul to one of the town's hotels. Paul hesitated. He rang Emma but there was no answer. Emma was probably out with the kids, organising ducklings, they decided.

So Margaret made her offer again. Paul looked at Margaret for a long moment—something intangible passing between them—and they'd walked out of the hospital together. Discussing bridesmaids and soccer, Dev thought grimly. Great combination.

Great match.

'I bet she'll sob at his funeral,' he told himself, and grimaced.

And then grinned. Yeah, OK, there was such a thing as love at first sight. After all, he ought to know.

What was he thinking?

This was dumb. And it was all Em's fault, he told himself, trying to drum up a bit of indignation as his car seemed to steer itself toward Emma. No.

Toward *his house*, he told himself. Not toward Em. Why should he steer toward Em?

She'd offered to free his future. She'd offered to stay here so he could do whatever he liked.

She'd introduced Paul to Margaret so his nice sensible marriage option was suddenly not such an option.

He hadn't actually decided to take up the option anyway.

And, if he was being truthful—not that he was in the mood for being truthful but he was a just man—he'd actually organised Paul to come here, he had to admit. He'd brought this on himself.

And then he thought, Yeah, I did ask Paul to come here, and Em will have seen the chemistry that's happened between them and she's probably feeling the same as me. Jilted. If Paul doesn't go back to her place tonight, how's she going to feel?

He didn't actually feel jilted, he conceded. And OK, the car was already headed in Em's direction. He'd just drive past…

Only he didn't. He drove in and the place was deserted. Beautifully deserted. The garden was lovely in the moonlight, cleared of undergrowth, its ancient trees exposed for the majestic sculptural things that they were.

He hardly saw the garden.

He was looking for Emma.

He opened the front door and the smell of beeswax and new paint assailed his nostrils in a heady mix, mingling with the smell of salt from the sea.

The furniture had been replaced, and more. One of the dads had made some simple frames and the kids had filled them with artwork of the most amazing kind. Bright, vivid seascapes, landscapes, moonlight over the water...

The house looked fabulous. Alive, vibrant, waiting for a family.

It wasn't going to get a family. Just Em. Em and her baby.

Em's bedroom door was open a crack. He shouldn't look in.

He did.

She wasn't there.

'Em?'

Silence.

Maybe she was down the beach. He grimaced. She'd had a big day. She should be in bed.

He wanted her to be in bed. For some reason there was a sense of urgency about seeing her. He wanted her to be here.

At the very least he wanted to know where she was.

He strolled down to the sand, or he tried to stroll. He tried to stop his feet from striding. He tried to stop himself from fretting.

Em? His eyes raked the moonlit cove.

Nothing.

'Em.' He stood and called into the night, and then cupped his hands and tried an Australian 'Cooee'.

More nothing.

He was worrying in earnest now. He took out his cellphone and rang Lorna.

'No, Dev dear, she's not here. Oh, but I have the dearest little ducklings. I've just run the bath…'

'Do you have any idea where she might be?'

'Check the bathroom. If she has ducklings… Ooh, you should see how they can swim.'

Clearly there wasn't a lot of sense to be gained from his mother.

Where was Emma?

If his mother was fretting about ducklings, maybe Em was, too. Maybe she'd walked up to the crash site to check there hadn't been some left.

Why would she? They were only ducklings.

This was Em they were talking about.

OK, he'd walk up there.

He stopped with the trying-not-to-hurry bit. He was moving with speed. Where the hell…?

Maybe she'd left town.

If she'd packed up and left she would have taken her gear and it was all here. If she'd gone out she would have locked the house.

If she was lying injured somewhere in the bush… If she'd gone into labor, had a hemorrhage, fallen off a cliff…

He was going nuts.

He went through the house on the way back to the road, checking the bathroom this time. If she was sitting in the bath playing with ducklings he was going to have to kill her.

Mind, the vision of Emma sitting in the bath with a few ducklings…

Cut it out, O'Halloran. How can you fantasize about a woman pregnant with your brother's baby?

How can you not?

She wasn't there.

'Em?'

He was feeling sick now. He was out the front door, heading for the road, and now he was running.

The night was warm and still and silent. The council guys had been at the crash site and had set up barricades, with warning lamps.

The road was deserted at this time of night.

No ducklings.

No Em.

Where the hell…? Where the hell…?

He leaned on a barricade and tried to force his mind to think. The house was open and the lights were on. She wouldn't have left it like that. She wouldn't!

He'd have to contact the cops. Get a few men out here. A search party.

Snakebite?

Hemorrhage?

His hands clenched. He stared out to sea. Nothing.

He cupped his hands in one last desperate measure, and yelled with everything he had.

'Emma!'

She damned near fell off her rock.

One minute she was sitting peacefully counting ducks in her head. Swinging her feet, gazing out at the moon over the water and trying not to think about the lump of rock that was digging into the very place where no one wanted a lump of rock.

The next minute the booming, male voice cracked the stillness, rolling like thunder out over the waves. 'Emma!' It came from right above her and it made her jump so hard that when she landed her lump of rock dug in even further.

Dev.

Dev was there.

Her heart did a little jump all by itself.

'Do you mind?' she said cautiously into the darkness. 'You're disturbing my babies.'

He was dreaming.

One minute he was yelling out over the waves,

despairing, hopeless. The next he was staring down the cliff, thinking he'd heard a ghost.

What had the voice said? 'You're disturbing my babies.'

Prosaic. Practical.

Em.

'What the hell?' he said, struggling to make his voice work. 'What the hell are you doing down there?'

He couldn't see her. He couldn't see anything. If he leaned out any further, the verge could give way. He'd plummet.

Had she plummeted?

'There are ducks,' the voice said.

He needed to think about that for a bit. 'I accept that there are ducks,' he said at last, goaded past the point where a man could endure anything. 'There are too many ducks. You mean you're down there, keeping them company?'

'Their crate was stuck below the high-water mark,' she said. 'They'd have drowned.'

'Ducks can swim.'

'Not in a crate.'

'So you decided to crawl down and save them.' He was still having a huge amount of trouble speaking. He was having a lot of trouble breathing.

'I didn't have much choice,' she said, indignant.

'You could have called me.'

'You were mending collar-bones,' she told him. 'With Margaret.'

'And Paul.' This conversation was crazy. Where was she?

'I think they've fallen in love,' she was saying. 'My boyfriend and your girlfriend. Isn't that nice?'

'Oh, for heaven's sake. This is crazy. Em, whereabouts—'

'Oh, that's right.' She sounded chastened. 'You don't believe in love at first sight.'

He wanted to shake her. He wanted to reach her! 'Em, where are you?'

'You can see where I am.'

'I can't see a thing.'

'Then maybe you should go find a torch,' she said helpfully. 'Actually, a torch might be great. Though come to think of it a rope might be even better. You could pull up the ducklings.'

'You climbed down there?'

'Yep. It was easy.'

'Right.' He peered over into the dark. Easy? She had to be kidding.

Maybe the moon had been slanting in from the east, giving her a view when she'd climbed down, but it was higher now and the cliff was in shadow. 'So you decided not to climb back up,' he said cautiously. 'Because there's not enough light?'

'Actually…'

'Actually, what?'

'A rock fell into the water,' she said, sounding a bit abashed. 'I sort of needed that rock. Maybe I'm a bit stuck.'

He drew in his breath. 'You're stuck. A rock fell in the water.' He found there was a level of fear in him that he hadn't known he was capable of feeling. 'Em, do you realise—?'

'But you're here now.' Damn, he could hear her smiling. 'And you're here without Margaret.'

'I might need Margaret to help pull you up.'

'Margaret wouldn't be good at pulling,' she said sagely.

'No, but she'd come with Paul, and—'

'We don't want Paul.'

His heart settled a little. Just a little. 'OK. We don't want Paul. But we need to get you up.'

'I agree.' She still sounded cheerful. 'Maybe I need a lifeboat.'

'Where the hell are you?'

'Go get a torch and you'll see.'

There was no choice.

'You sure you're safe? You're above the high-water mark?'

'Yep, and so are my babies.'

'You're not hurt.'

'No, but I'm a bit worried about the ducklings. I can't see.'

'Em—'

'Just hurry up,' she told him. 'Oh, and, Dev?'

'Yes?' He was already moving.

'If you're bringing a torch from the house, there's no chance of bringing me back a lamington at the same time, is there? The fridge is full of food. I'm really, really hungry and I bet even my babies would like a bit of lamington.'

She was cramping.

Her legs hurt.

Her backside hurt.

OK, all of her hurt.

She didn't care. Dev was coming.

With lamingtons.

He moved with speed and with precision, and thankfully he knew what he was doing.

Once, a long time ago, he and Corey had fished from the cliffs where Em was now stranded. They'd clambered down the rockface and caught bream and taylor and whiting and had brought them home to their long-suffering mother to clean and to cook.

Then, in the middle of a long hot school holiday, they'd caught a shark. A gummy shark. It was better eating than most fish he knew. Even his too-busy dad had been excited.

But it had caused a problem. The thing had weighed a ton.

So he and Corey and their Dad had fashioned a sling, then rigged up a harness and ropes and pulleys so the shark could be hauled up the cliff while Corey rose alongside it, guiding it over bumps and keeping it pristine for vital photographs up the top.

It had worked brilliantly. Dev remembered the day with huge pleasure. His father had come home for lunch and stayed, and by the time the shark had been raised, half his father's patients had been on top of the cliff, cheering.

After that episode, cliff-climbing had gained an excitement all its own. They'd used the harness and pulleys many times—to haul up excellent pieces of driftwood that had been washed under the cliffs, to rescue a canoe that had lost a paddle, to simply play on the rockface and practise their rock-climbing skills.

Corey had been well then. They'd still been a family.

All this Dev thought as he ran, but what he needed to know was whether the equipment was still in the shed. His mother had thrown out so much. If it wasn't there…

It was. Ropes, pulleys, harness.

Torch. Two torches.

He started back—and then hesitated. Went back to the kitchen. Grabbed half a dozen lamingtons and shoved them in his pockets. And grinned.

They'd be squashed, but something told him Emma wouldn't care.

'He'll be here soon,' she told the ducklings. 'Don't get hypothermia.'

Cheep.

'Don't any of you die.'

Cheep.

He's coming.

'Em? *Em?*' She could hear the fear.

'I'm still here. Don't get your knickers in a twist. Did you bring my lamingtons?'

There was a small expletive, telling her what he thought of lamingtons. She laughed, breathless. Lit up. Her legs almost forgot to cramp.

'I told you,' she told the ducklings. 'He's my thoroughly dependable Dev. Our lamingtons are on their way.'

There was a clatter of stones, an oath, a beam of light shining down, just missing her.

'Where the hell are you?' he demanded.

'You keep asking that. I'm under the overhang.'

'I might have known you'd be under the overhang.' Exasperation. Something more. A tenderness that took her breath away.

She fought to stay pragmatic. 'I know. I have no consideration. I need a good talking-to.'

'You need more than that.'

'Like what?' she asked hopefully. 'What do I need?'

'I haven't decided yet,' he said, goaded. 'Just sit. Wait.'

'Yes, sir.'

He should wring her neck.

Of all the stupid, dangerous, crazy escapades a pregnant woman doctor could embark on, this would have to take the cake. For a doctor to forget her training and do such a dumb, mad thing…. It was unthinkable. The first medical priority was to avoid danger yourself. She'd climbed down there without ropes!

She should go back to medical school.

Medical school was safe. She'd be safe if she was anywhere but here.

It was so damned dark. Why couldn't he see her?

He'd attached his rope to a tree trunk, a gum, four feet in diameter at its base. Safe enough. He was climbing down hand over hand. Careful. Careful.

How the hell had she done this without ropes? Emma.

He definitely intended to wring her neck.

'Dev.'

She was right under him. He couldn't peer down now. He could only lower himself slowly, searching for toeholds in the dark.

'There's room on my ledge,' she said softly, unsteadily, from not very far below him. 'If I squash up.'

'Then squash up.'

'Yes, sir.'

Her hand was on his leg, gently touching, guiding.

She was really there, he thought as he felt her tentative touch. Part of him couldn't believe it.

He'd wring her neck. He'd…

She was tugging him down. He was nearly there. Her hand was on his arm. He was finding her ledge, she was shoving along, hauling him against her.

He'd reached her.

He was going to have to wring her neck.

His arms were around her neck.

She was in his arms.

He was kissing her as if there was no tomorrow.

His Em.

He'd come home.

Afterwards, a long time afterwards, when there was room and space between them for words, gentle words whispered against each other while they held tight, merged, loved, he remembered his intention.

'You deserve to have your neck wrung.'

'You, too,' she whispered. 'What took you so long?'

'What?'

'We could have died of hunger.' She chuckled and snuggled closer. 'Come to think of it, we still could. Do you have those lamingtons?'

'I do.'

'My hero.'

'I put them in my front pocket,' he said cautiously. 'You may just have squashed them when you lunged at my body.'

'No lamington ever died in a nobler cause,' she told him, and he could hear the smile in her voice. 'I'll eat them squashed.'

'You really are OK?'

'I really am OK.'

'No cramps?'

'Cramps everywhere, but no contractions. This baby's clearly destined to be a mountaineer.'

'Corey loved climbing cliffs.'

'There you go, then,' she said placidly. She dug into the pocket he was opening and retrieved the better part of a lamington. Or…if not the better part, at least a part.

He sat and watched her eat it. The moonlight was glinting upward from the water, playing on her face. She ate and he just watched. And as he did, things settled. The world righted on its axis.

His brother, his beloved brother, had died. The disease that had killed him had taken him from his family long before his death, but a part of him, the part of Corey that must have stayed intact during that awful time, had found this magical chit of a girl, this lovely laughing woman. He'd given her a child.

And in a way, he'd brought her home.

Now Emma was embracing more than Corey's family. She was embracing him. Loving him.

Corey had rescued Emma. Emma had tried to rescue Corey, and on that awful last night, as she'd used her body to comfort him, she'd given him the gift of a child. Corey had given all of them the gift of a child.

And now…the two of them, the spirit of his brother and this elf, this wonderful crazy woman who Corey had found, had in turn rescued him.

Emma was his, he knew, and it was suddenly a triumphant, exultant burst of recognition. The doubts he'd had, the awful greyness that had been part of the grief and guilt of Corey's loss, fell away.

Sure, he'd love Corey until the day he died.

But now… He still had Corey, he thought. He and Em could talk about Corey with love. Corey would be a part of them for ever. Corey would live on—in his mother's joy over her grandchild, in their exploits and their happiness as they turned this place into a family home, as they walked into their future together.

'What?' Emma was asking, a trifle breathless. 'Why are you looking at me like that?'

'I love you.'

'Really?'

'Really.'

'You know, I hoped that might happen,' she whispered, and she leaned forward and kissed him again, lightly this time, on the lips and then on the forehead. It was a gentle claim. A blessing. Then she drew back. 'But why are you looking at me like that?' she demanded again. 'Like I've got co-conut on my nose.'

'You have got coconut on your nose.'

'Rats.' She put out her tongue and licked.

Her tongue reached the tip of her nose.

'That's impossible,' he said, and flicked on the torch. 'Do it again.'

She did it again.

'Is there no end to your talents?'

'Nope,' she said smugly. 'You should hear me sing in the shower. You haven't lived until you've heard me sing in the shower.'

'Corey must have loved you,' he said.

'Corey loved you,' she told him. 'So we're even. Doubly blessed.'

'Will we call this baby Corey?'

'Nope.' She thought about it and shook her head in decision. 'That's heavy. Corey would have hated that. We'll call a duckling Corey.' She frowned. 'Speaking of ducklings...'

'Give them some lamingtons. Distract them. I want to kiss their mother.'

'They need water.'

'They have an ocean six feet away.'

'You know what I mean.'

'Shut up, Dr O'Halloran, and be kissed.'

'If you're going to be bossy...'

'I'm going to be bossy. You've had a very bad shock, Dr O'Halloran. You require comfort.'

'Is that a prescription?'

'Doctor's orders.'

'Really?' she asked happily, snuggling into him again. 'Well, if that's the case I can't argue. Can I?'

There was no room for response. And no need. There was no argument at all.

It was some party.

It was the dedication of the Kyle and Corey memorial garden.

It was the christening of Caroline Lorna Louise O'Halloran.

It was the wedding of Devlin O'Halloran to Emma O'Halloran.

The whole town was there. Of course they were, crammed into their beautiful garden that they all now seemed to own.

There were ten flower-girls and eleven page-boys. Somewhere on the Gravitron of Doom—at Emma's promised Adventure World pay-day at the end of the school holidays—the kids had asked Dev if they could all be flower-girls or page-boys, and Dev had staggered off the ride to a laughing, waiting Emma and had agreed that anyone could be anything they wanted.

So there were ten pink frilly dresses and eleven small dinner suits, made by the Karington Mothers' Club with pleasure and with pride, clothing twenty-one of Karington's finest young men and women.

There were special jobs, though. Katy was chief flower-girl. With brand-new contact lenses and a well-behaving spleen, her job was to head the pack and take care of Emma's bouquet.

Jodie and Suzy were second in line. They carried the rose petals.

The rest looked beautiful. And important. And happy.

Someone had decided that this wasn't enough, though. There were also ducks. Thirty or so sleek young ducks were waddling round the garden, each sporting bright pink ribbons in bridal splendour. At the end of the day Ruby would collect them and finally take them to their new home.

But not yet. There were formalities to take place first.

There were also other roles to be filled.

Best man?

That would be Margaret.

Chief bridesmaid? Paul.

'Our best friends,' Dev had said, smiling. 'Choose which job you want.' So they'd chuckled and smiled at each other and chosen.

No one minded. This was one crazy wedding.

The bride was given away by her mother-in-law.

'No one else is going to do it,' Lorna declared. 'I'm so happy I could bust.'

She wasn't going to bust—though if the size of the wedding feast was an indicator, they all could.

The garden was a mass of colour. In these few weeks so much had happened. Everyone had worked here now. There were two wonderful seats up on the facing bluffs—made by the guy who'd driven the school bus.

'I was hopeless during the accident,' he'd said. 'Let me do this.' And in his work he'd found a measure of peace.

As they all had.

This was perfect.

Everything was perfect.

'Don't you want to go to America?' Emma had asked, and Dev had held her close and kissed her hair and told her she had to be crazy to suggest such a thing.

'Why would I possibly want to go to America?'

'Your work...'

'I have work to do here. Such work. You and I can make the best medical team in the southern hemisphere.'

'But—'

'No buts.'

And now he was waiting. Under the arch of crimson roses, he was waiting for his bride.

The town was watching.

Up on the veranda stood Harriet, their obstetrician. She was holding Caroline Lorna Louise, four weeks old. Caroline might be too young to be a flower-girl, but she was old enough to gaze upward with her father's eyes, with Dev's eyes, and take in this strange, new, wonderful world.

The music started. A children's choir, led by Colin. Backed by the town band.

All eyes went to the front door.

Out came Emma. Tremulous, beautiful.

Her cream silk dress had a full-circle, free-flowing skirt. Her bodice was scooped low and laced with pale pink ribbons. Her wild curls were tamed, threaded with a wreath of pink rosebuds Kyle's mother had fashioned for her that morning.

Lorna held her hand and beamed and beamed and beamed.

And Dev's heart turned over.

His love. His brother's gift to him. His life.

She was walking toward him, smiling and smiling, but he couldn't smile back.

His Emma. His perfect Emma.

She reached him. She took his hand and finally, finally he let himself believe that it was real.

It wasn't time yet—but what the heck? He took her hand from Lorna—and he kissed her. The kiss went on and on, while around them people cheered and laughed and surreptitiously wiped away a few tears.

'My love,' he whispered. 'My love.'

'You want to get married?' she murmured, and at last he smiled.

'Why not?'

So they turned together, to be made one.

The world held its breath.

One after the other they made their vows.

'With this ring I thee wed. With my body I thee worship. Till death do us part.'

And then there was a smile and a gentle blessing.

'I now pronounce you man and wife.'

They turned to those who loved them. They smiled. Hand in hand. Man and wife.

God was in his heaven; all was right with the world.

The ghosts of this place were at peace.

For ever.

MEDICAL ROMANCE™

Large Print

Titles for the next six months…

May

THE NURSE'S CHRISTMAS WISH   Sarah Morgan
THE CONSULTANT'S CHRISTMAS PROPOSAL
                 Kate Hardy
NURSE IN A MILLION   Jennifer Taylor
A CHILD TO CALL HER OWN   Gill Sanderson

June

GIFT OF A FAMILY   Sarah Morgan
CHRISTMAS ON THE CHILDREN'S WARD   Carol Marinelli
THE LIFE SAVER   Lilian Darcy
THE NOBLE DOCTOR   Gill Sanderson

July

HER CELEBRITY SURGEON   Kate Hardy
COMING BACK FOR HIS BRIDE   Abigail Gordon
THE NURSE'S SECRET SON   Amy Andrews
THE SURGEON'S RESCUE MISSION   Dianne Drake

MILLS & BOON®

Live the emotion

0406 LP 2P P1 Medical

MEDICAL ROMANCE™

Large Print

August

NEEDED: FULL-TIME FATHER   Carol Marinelli
THE SURGEON'S ENGAGEMENT WISH   Alison Roberts
SHEIKH SURGEON   Meredith Webber
THE EMERGENCY DOCTOR'S PROPOSAL   Joanna Neil

September

HIS SECRET LOVE-CHILD   Marion Lennox
HER HONOURABLE PLAYBOY   Kate Hardy
THE SURGEON'S PREGNANCY SURPRISE
    Laura MacDonald
IN HIS LOVING CARE   Jennifer Taylor

October

THE DOCTOR'S UNEXPECTED PROPOSAL
    Alison Roberts
THE DOCTOR'S SURPRISE BRIDE   Fiona McArthur
A KNIGHT TO HOLD ON TO   Lucy Clark
HER BOSS AND PROTECTOR   Joanna Neil

MILLS & BOON®

Live the emotion

0406 LP 2P P2 Medical